NOW THAT MAGICK HAS FOUND ME,
MY LIFE WILL NEVER BE THE SAME.

# Book Two

# sweep

*Cate Tiernan*

# THE COVEN

**speak**

An Imprint of Penguin Group (USA) Inc.

All quoted materials in this work were created by the author.
Any resemblance to existing works is accidental.

The Coven

SPEAK
Published by the Penguin Group
Penguin Group (USA) Inc., 345 Hudson Street, New York, New York 10014, U.S.A.
Penguin Group (Canada), 90 Eglinton Avenue East, Suite 700, Toronto, Ontario, Canada M4P 2Y3
(a division of Pearson Penguin Canada Inc.)
Penguin Books Ltd, 80 Strand, London WC2R 0RL, England
Penguin Ireland, 25 St Stephen's Green, Dublin 2, Ireland (a division of Penguin Books Ltd)
Penguin Group (Australia), 250 Camberwell Road, Camberwell, Victoria 3124, Australia
(a division of Pearson Australia Group Pty Ltd)
Penguin Books India Pvt Ltd, 11 Community Centre, Panchsheel Park, New Delhi - 110 017, India
Penguin Group (NZ), 67 Apollo Drive, Mairangi Bay, Auckland 1311, New Zealand
(a division of Pearson New Zealand Ltd)
Penguin Books (South Africa) (Pty) Ltd, 24 Sturdee Avenue, Rosebank, Johannesburg 2196, South Africa

Registered Offices: Penguin Books Ltd, 80 Strand, London WC2R 0RL, England

Published by Puffin Books, a division of Penguin Young Readers Group, 2001
This edition published by Speak, an imprint of Penguin Group (USA) Inc., 2007

1   3   5   7   9   10   8   6   4   2

Produced by 17th Street Productions,
an Alloy company
151 West 26th Street
New York, NY 10001

17th Street Productions and associated logos
are trademarks and/or registered trademarks of Alloy, Inc.

Speak ISBN 978-0-14-240987-9

Printed in the United States of America

*To N. and P.,*
*who have brought so much magic into my life*

# Prologue

I was dancing in the atmosphere, surrounded by stars, seeing motes of energy whizzing past me like microscopic comets. I could see the entire universe, all at once; every particle, every smile, every fly, every grain of sand was revealed to me and was infinitely beautiful.

When I breathed in, I breathed in the very essence of life, and I breathed out white light. It was beautiful, more than beautiful, but I didn't have the words to express it even to myself. I understood everything; I understood my place in the universe; I understood the path I had to follow.

Then I smiled and blinked and breathed out again, and I was standing in a darkened graveyard with nine high school friends, and tears were running down my face.

"Are you okay?" Robbie asked in concern, coming over to me.

At first it seemed he was speaking gibberish, but then I understood what he had said, and I nodded.

"It was so beautiful," I said lamely, my voice breaking. I felt unbearably diminished after my vision. I reached my finger out to touch Robbie's cheek. My finger left a warm pink line where it touched, and Robbie rubbed his cheek, looking confused.

The vases of flowers were on the altar, and I walked toward them, mesmerized by their beauty and also the overwhelming sadness of the flowers' deaths. I touched one bud, and it opened beneath my hand, blooming in death as it hadn't been allowed to in life. I heard Raven gasp and knew that Bree and Beth and Matt backed away from me then.

Then Cal was next to me. "Quit touching things," he said quietly, smiling. "Lie down and ground yourself."

He guided me to an open spot within our circle, and I lay down on my back, feeling the pulsing life of the earth centering me, easing the energy from me, making me feel more normal. My perceptions focused, and I saw the coven clearly, saw the candles, the stars, the fruit as themselves again and not as pulsing blobs of energy.

"What's happening to me?" I whispered. Cal sat cross-legged and lifted my head onto his lap, stroking my hair strewn across his legs. Robbie knelt next to him. Ethan, Beth, and Sharon circled closer, peering over his shoulder at me as if I were a museum display. Jenna was holding Matt around his waist, as if she were afraid. Raven and Bree were the farthest back, and Bree looked wide-eyed and solemn.

"You made magick," Cal said, gazing at me with those endless golden eyes. "You're a blood witch."

My eyes opened wider as his face slowly blotted out the moon above me. With his eyes looking deeply into mine, he touched my mouth with his, and with a sense of shock I realized he was kissing me. My arms felt heavy as I moved them up to encircle his neck, and then I was kissing him back, and we were joined, and the magick crackled all around us.

In that moment of sheer happiness I didn't question what being a blood witch meant to me or my family or what Cal and I being together meant to Bree or Raven or Robbie or anyone else. It would be my first lesson in magick, and it would be hard learned: seeing the big picture, not just a part of it.

# 1

# After Samhain

*This book is given to my incandescent one, my fire fairy, Bradhadair, on her fourteenth birthday. Welcome to Belwicket. With love from Mathair.*

><

This book is private. Keep out.

Imbolc, 1976

Here's an easy spell to start my Book of Shadows. I got it from Betts Towson, except I use black candles and she uses blue.

### To Get Rid of a Bad Habit

1. Light altar candles.
2. Light black candle. Say: "This holds me back. No more will I do it. No more is it part of me."
3. Light white candle. Say: "This is my might and my courage and my victory. This battle is already won."

4.  Picture in your mind the bad habit you want to break. Picture yourself free from it. After a few minutes of imagining victory, put out the black candle, then the white candle.
5.  Repeat a week later if necessary. Best done during a waning moon.


I did this last Thursday as part of my initiation. I haven't bitten my nails since. —— Bradhadair


I woke slowly on the day after Samhain. I tried to resist the light behind my eyes, but soon I was awake, and there was nothing I could do about it.

My room was barely light. It was the first day of November, and the warmth of autumn had leached away. I stretched, then was flooded with memories and sensations so strong that I sat straight up in bed.

Shivering, I saw again Cal leaning over me, kissing me. Me, kissing Cal back, my arms around his neck, his hair soft beneath my fingers. The connection we made, our magick, the electricity, the sparks, the way the universe swirled around us . . . I am a blood witch, I thought. I am a blood witch, and Cal loves me, and I love Cal. And that's the way it is.

The night before, I'd had my first kiss, found my first love. I had also betrayed my best friend, created a rift in my new coven, and realized my parents had lied to me my whole life.

All of this happened on Samhain, October 31, the witches' New Year. My new year, my new life.

I lay back down in bed, the coziness of my flannel sheets and comforter reassuring. Last night I had seen my dreams come true. Now I knew, with a coldness in my stomach, I would pay the price for them. I felt much older than sixteen.

Blood witch, I thought. Cal says that's what I am, and after last night, after what I did, how can I doubt it? It must be true. I am a blood witch. In my veins flows blood that has been inherited from thousands of years of magick making, thousands of years of witches intermarrying. I'm one of them, from one of the Seven Great Clans: Rowanwand, Wyndenkell, Leapvaughn, Vikroth, Brightendale, Burnhide, and Woodbane.

But which one? Rowanwand, both teachers and hoarders of knowledge? Wyndenkell, the expert spell writers? Vikroth? The Vikroths were magickal warriors, later related to Vikings. I smiled. I didn't feel very warrior-like.

The Leapvaughns were mischief makers, joke players. The Burnhide clan focused on doing magick with gems, crystals, and metals, and the Brightendales were the medical clan, using the magick of plants to heal. Or . . . there was Woodbane. I shivered. There was no way I was of the dark clan, the ones who wanted power at any cost, the ones who battled and betrayed their fellow clans for control of land, of magickal power, of knowledge.

I considered it. Of the seven great clans, if I was in fact from one of them, I felt most like the Brightendales, the healers. I had discovered that I loved plants, that they spoke to me, that using their magickal powers came naturally to me. I hugged myself, smiling. A Brightendale. A real blood witch.

Which means my parents must also be blood witches, I thought. It was a stunning notion. It made me wonder why we'd been going to church every Sunday for as long as I could remember. I mean, I liked my church. I liked going to services. They seemed beautiful and traditional and comforting. But Wicca felt more natural.

I sat up in bed again. Two images kept coming at me: Cal leaning over me, his golden eyes locked on mine. And Bree, my best friend: the shock and pain on her face as she saw Cal and me together. The accusation, hurt, desire. Rage.

What have I done? I wondered.

I heard my parents downstairs in the kitchen, starting coffee, unloading the dishwasher. Flopping back down in bed, I listened to the familiar sounds: Not every single thing in my life had changed last night.

Someone opened the front door to get the paper. Today was Sunday, which meant church, followed by brunch at the Widow's Diner. Seeing Cal later? Would I talk to him? Were we going out now, a couple? He had kissed me in front of everyone—what had it meant? Was Cal Blaire, beautiful Cal Blaire, really attracted to me, Morgan Rowlands? Me, with my flat chest and my assertive nose? Me, who guys never looked at twice?

I stared up at my ceiling as if the answers were written on the cracked plaster. When the door to my room burst open, I jumped.

"Can you explain this?" my mom asked. Her brown eyes were wide, her mouth tight, with deeply carved lines around it. She held up a small stack of books, tied with string. They were the books I had left at Bree's house because I knew my parents didn't want me to have them, my books on Wicca, the Seven Great Clans, the history of witchcraft. A note attached to the books said in big letters: "Morgan—You left these at my house. Thought you might need them." Sitting up, I realized this was Bree's revenge.

"I thought we had an understanding," Mom said, her voice rising. She leaned out my bedroom door and yelled, "Sean!"

I swung my legs out of bed. The floor was cold, and I pushed my feet into my slippers.

"Well?" Mom's voice was a decibel louder, and my dad came into my room, looking alarmed.

"Mary Grace?" he said. "What's going on?"

Mom held up the books as if they were a dead rat. "These were on the front porch!" she said. "Look at the note!"

She turned back to me. "What do you think you're doing?" she demanded, incredulous. "When I said I didn't want these books in my house, that didn't mean I wanted you reading them in someone else's house! You knew what I meant, Morgan!"

"Mary Grace," my dad soothed, taking the books from her. He read their titles silently.

My younger sister, Mary K., padded into the room, still in her plaid patchwork pajamas. "What's going on?" she said, pushing her hair out of her eyes. No one answered.

I tried to think fast. "Those books aren't dangerous or illegal. And I wanted to read them. I'm not a child—I'm sixteen. Anyway, I was respecting your wishes not to have them in the house."

"Morgan," my dad said, sounding uncharacteristically stern. "It's not just having the books in the house, and you know it. We explained that as Catholics, we feel that witchcraft is wrong. It may not be illegal, but it's blasphemous."

"You are sixteen," Mom put in. "Not eighteen. That means you are still a child." Her face was flushed, her hair unbrushed. I could see silver strands among the red. It hit me that in four years she would be fifty. That suddenly seemed old.

"You live under our roof," Mom continued tightly. "We support you. When you're eighteen and you move out and get a job, you can have whatever books you want, read whatever you want. But while you're in this house, what we say goes."

I started to get angry. Why were they acting this way?

But before I said anything, a verse came into my head. Leash my anger, calm my words. Speak in love and do no hurt.

Where did that come from? I wondered vaguely. But whatever its origin, it felt right. I said it to myself three times and felt my emotions ratchet down.

"I understand," I said. Suddenly I felt powerful and confident. I looked at my parents and my sister. "But Mom, it isn't that easy," I explained gently. "And you know why; I know you do. I'm a witch. I was born a witch. And if I was, then you were, too."

# 2

# Different

*December 14, 1976.*

*Circle last night at the currachdag on the west cliffs. Fifteen of us in all, including me, Angus, Mannannan, the rest of Belwicket, and two students, Tara and Cliff. It was cold, and a fine rain fell. Standing around the great heap of peat, we did some healing for old Mrs. Paxham, down to the village, who's been ailing. I felt the cumhachd, the power, in my fingers, in my arms, and I was happy and danced for hours. — Bradhadair*

My mother looked like she was about to have a stroke. Dad's mouth dropped open. Mary K. stared at me, her brown eyes wide.

Mom's mouth worked as if she was trying to speak but couldn't form the words. Her face was pale, and I wanted to tell her to sit down, to take it easy. But I kept silent. I knew this was a turning point for us, and I couldn't back down.

"What did you say?" Her voice was a raw whisper.

"I said I'm a witch," I repeated calmly, though inside, my nerves were stretched and taut. "I'm a blood witch, a genetic witch. And if I am, you two must be also."

"What are you talking about?" Mary K. said. "There's no such thing as a genetic witch! God, next you'll be telling us there are vampires and werewolves." She looked at me in disbelief, her plaid pajamas seeming young and innocent. Suddenly I felt guilty, as if I had brought evil into the house. But that wasn't true, was it? All I had brought into the house was me, a part of me.

I raised my hand, then let it fall, not knowing what to say.

"I can't believe you," Mary K. said. "What are you trying to do?" She gestured toward our parents.

Ignoring her, Mom said faintly, "You're not a witch."

I almost snorted. "Mom, please. That's like saying I'm not a girl or I'm not human. Of course I'm a witch, and you know it. You've always known it."

"Morgan, just stop it!" Mary K. pleaded. "You're freaking me out. You want to read witch books? Fine. Read witch books, light candles, whatever. But quit saying you're really a witch. That's bullshit!"

Mom snapped her gaze to Mary K., startled.

"'Scuse me," Mary K. muttered.

"I'm sorry, Mary K.," I said. "It's not something I wanted to happen. But it's true." A thought occurred to me. "You must be one, too," I said, finding that idea fascinating. I looked up at her, excited. "Mary K., you must be a witch, too!"

"*She is not a witch!*" my mom shrieked, and I stopped, frozen by the sound of her voice. She looked enraged, the veins in her neck standing out, her face flushed. "You leave her out of it!"

"But—," I began.

"Mary K. is not a witch, Morgan," my dad said harshly.

I shook my head. "But she has to be," I said. "I mean, it's genetic. And if I am, and you are, then . . ."

"Nobody is a witch," my mom said shortly, not meeting my eyes. "Certainly not Mary Kathleen."

They were in denial. But why?

"Mom, it's okay. Really. More than okay. Being a witch is a wonderful thing," I said, thinking back to the feelings I'd had last night. "It's like being—"

"Will you stop?" Mom burst out. "Why are you doing this? Why can't you just listen to us?" She sounded on the verge of tears, and I was getting angry again.

"I can't listen to you because you're wrong!" I said loudly. "Why are you denying all of this?"

*"We're not witches!"* my mom screeched, practically rattling my windows.

She glared at me. My dad's mouth was open, and Mary K. looked miserable. I felt the first hint of fear.

"Oh," I snapped. "I guess I'm a witch, but you're not, right?" I snorted, furious at their stubbornness, their lies. "Then what?" I crossed my arms and looked at them. "Was I adopted?"

Silence. Long moments of the clock ticking, the thin, scratchy sound of elm twigs brushing my windowpanes. My heartbeat seemed to go into slow motion. Mom groped for my desk chair, then sank into it heavily. My dad shifted from foot to foot, looking over my left shoulder at nothing. Mary K. stared at all of us.

"What?" I tried to smile. "What? What are you saying? I'm *adopted?*"

"Of course you're not adopted!" said Mary K., looking at Mom and Dad for their agreement.

Silence.

Inside me, a wall came crashing down, and I saw what lay behind it: a whole world I had never dreamed of, a world in which I was adopted, not biologically related to my family. My throat closed and my stomach clenched, and I was afraid I was going to throw up. But I had to know.

I pushed past Mary K. into the hallway, then thundered down the steps two at a time. I tore around the corner, hearing my parents on the steps behind me. In the family office I yanked open my dad's files, where he keeps things like insurance papers, our passports, their marriage license . . . birth certificates.

Breathing hard, I flipped through files on car insurance, the house's AC system, our new water heater. My file read *Morgan*. I pulled it out just as my parents came into the office.

"Morgan! Stop it!" said Dad.

Ignoring him, I rifled through immunization records, school reports, my social security card.

There it was. My birth certificate. I picked it up and scanned it. *Birthday, November 23.* Correct. *Weight, eight pounds, ten ounces.*

My mom reached around me and snatched the birth certificate out of my hand. As if in a slapstick movie, I snatched it back. She held tight with both hands, and the paper ripped.

Dropping to my knees, I hunched over my half on the floor, protecting it till I could read it. *Age of mother: 23.* No.

That was wrong because Mom had been thirty before she had me.

Then the edges of the paper grew cloudy as my eyes locked onto four words: *Mother's name: Maeve Riordan.*

I blinked, reading it again and again at the speed of light. *Maeve Riordan. Mother's name: Maeve Riordan.*

Mechanically I read down to the bottom of my torn page, expecting to see my mom's real name, Mary Grace Rowlands, somewhere. Anywhere.

Shocked, I looked up at my mother. She seemed to have aged ten years in the last half hour. My dad, behind her, was tight-lipped and silent.

I held up the paper, my brain misfiring. "What does this mean?" I asked stupidly.

My parents didn't answer, and I stared at them. My fears came crashing down on me in hard waves. Suddenly I couldn't bear to be with them. I had to get away. Scrambling to my feet, I rushed from the room, colliding with Mary K., almost knocking her down. The torn scrap of paper fluttered from my fingers as I pushed through the kitchen door and grabbed the keys to my car. I raced outside as if the devil were chasing me.

# 3

# Find Me

May 14, 1977

Going to school is more a bother these days than anything else. It's spring, everything's blooming, I'm out gathering luibh — plants — for my spells, and then I have to get to school and learn English. What for? I live in Ireland. Anyway, I'm fifteen now, old enough to quit. Tonight's a full moon, so I'll do a scrying spell to see the future. I hope it will tell me whether I should stay in school or no. Scrying is hard to control, though.

There's something else I want to scry for: Angus. Is he my mùirn beatha dàn? On Beltane he pulled me behind the straw man and kissed me and said he loves me. I don't know how I feel about him. I thought I liked David O'Hearn. But he's not one of us — not a blood witch — and Angus is. For each of us there's only one other they should be with: their mùirn beatha dàn. For Ma, it was Da. Who is mine? Angus says it's him. If it's him, I have no choice, do I?

To scry: I don't use water overmuch — water is the easiest but also the least reliable. You know, a shallow bowl of clear water, gaze at it under the open sky or near a window. You'll see things easily enough, but it's wrong so often, I think it's just asking for trouble.

The best way to scry is with an enchanted leug, like bloodstone or hematite, or a crystal, but these are hard to lay your hands on. They give the most truth, but brace yourself for things you might not want to see or know. Stone scrying is good for seeing things as they are happening someplace else, like checking on a loved one or an enemy in battle.

I scry with fire, usually. Fire is unpredictable. But I'm made of fire, we are one, and so she speaks to me. With fire scrying, if I see something, it can be past, present, or future. Of course the future stuff is only one possible future. But what I see in fire is true, as true as can be.

I love the fire.

— Bradhadair

I ran across the frost-stiffened grass, which crunched lightly under my slippers. The front door opened behind me, but I was already sliding onto the freezing vinyl front seat of my white '71 Valiant, Das Boot, and cranking the engine.

"Morgan!" my dad yelled as I squealed out of our driveway, the car lurching like a boat on rough waters. Then I roared forward, watching my parents on our front lawn in my rearview mirror. Mom was sinking to the ground; Dad was trying to hold her up. I burst into tears as I wheeled too fast onto Riverdale.

Sobbing, I dashed my tears away with one hand, then wiped my nose on my sleeve. I turned on Das Boot's heater, but of course it took forever for the engine to warm up.

I was turning onto Bree's street before I remembered that we were no longer friends. If she hadn't left those books on my porch, I wouldn't know I was adopted. If Cal hadn't come between us, she would never have left the books on my porch.

I cried harder, shaking with sobs, and spun into a sloppy U-turn right before I reached her driveway. Then I hit the gas and drove, my only destination to be away, away.

The next time my vision cleared, I had managed to fish a battered box of tissues from beneath the front seat. Damp, crumpled ones littered the passenger side and covered the floor. I had ended up heading north, out of town. The road followed a low valley, and early fog clung heavily to the asphalt. Das Boot plowed through it like a brick thrown through clouds. In the distance I saw a large, dark shadow off to the side of the road. It was the willow oak that we had parked under just last night, for Samhain. Where I had parked the first time I did a circle with Cal, weeks before. When magick had come into my life.

Without thinking, I swung my car off the road and bumped across the field, rolling to a stop beneath the oak's low-hanging branches. Here I was hidden by fog, by the tree. I turned off my engine, leaned against the steering wheel, and tried to stop crying.

*Adopted.* Every instance, every example of my being different from my family reared up in my face and mocked me. Yesterday they had been only family jokes—how the three of them are larks and I'm a night owl, how they're unnaturally cheerful and I'm grumpy. How Mom and Mary K. are curvy and cute and I'm thin and intense. Today those jokes caused waves of pain as I remembered them one by one.

"Dammit! Dammit! Dammit!" I shouted, banging my fists against the hard metal steering wheel. "Dammit!" I whacked the wheel until my hands were numb, until I had gone through every curse I knew, until my throat was raw.

Then I wept again, lying down in the front seat. I don't know how long I was there, cocooned in my car in the mist. From time to time I turned on the heater to stay warm. The windows fogged and steamed with my tears.

Gradually my sobs degenerated into shaky hiccups and the occasional shudder. Oh, Cal, I thought. I need Cal. As soon as I thought that, a rhyme came into my head: *In my mind I see you here. In my pain I need you near. Find me, trace me, where I be. Come here, come here, now to me.*

I didn't know where it came from, but by now I was getting used to the arrival of strange thoughts. I felt calmer hearing it, so I said it over and over again. I draped my arm over my eyes, praying desperately I would wake up in bed at home to find it had all been a nightmare.

Minutes later I jumped when someone tapped on the passenger's-side window. My eyes snapped open, and I sat up, then cleared a space on the glass to see Cal, looking sleepy and rumpled and amazingly beautiful.

"You called?" he said, and my heart filled with sunlight. "Let me in—it's freezing out here."

It worked, I thought in awe. I called him with my thoughts. Magick.

I opened the door and moved over. He slid onto the front seat next to me, and it was amazingly natural to reach out, to feel his arms come around me.

"What's the matter?" he said, his voice muffled against my hair. "What's going on?" He held me away from him and searched my tear-blotched face with his eyes.

"I'm adopted!" I blurted out. "This morning I told my mom that I'm a blood witch, so she must be, and my dad, and my sister. They said no, it wasn't true. So I ran downstairs to see my birth certificate, and it had another woman's name—not my mother's."

I started crying again, even though I was embarrassed to have him see me like this. He pulled me closer and held my head to his shoulder. It was so comforting that I stopped crying again almost immediately.

"That's a hard way to find out." He kissed my temple, and a tiny shiver of pleasure raced up my spine. It's a miracle, I thought: He still loves me, even today. It wasn't a dream.

He pulled back, and we looked at each other in the hazy light. I couldn't get over how beautiful he was. His skin was smooth and tan, even in November. His hair was thick beneath my fingers, dark and streaked with warm shades the color of walnuts. His eyes were surrounded by blunt, black lashes, with irises of a gold so fiery, they almost seemed to radiate heat.

I felt self-conscious as I realized he was examining me the same way I examined him. A tiny smile quirked the corner of his lips. "Left in a hurry, did you?"

That was when I realized I was still in my oversize football jersey and an ancient pair of my dad's long johns, complete with flap in front. A large pair of brown, furry bear-feet slippers were on my feet. Cal reached down and tickled their claws. I thought about the silky matching outfits that Bree wears to sleep in, and with a pang and an indrawn breath I remembered she'd told me that she and Cal had gone to bed. I searched his eyes, wondering if it was true, wondering if I could bear knowing for sure.

But he was here now. With me.

"You're the best thing I've seen all morning," Cal said softly, stroking my arm. "I'm glad you called me. I missed you last night, after I went home."

I looked down, thinking of him lying in his big, romantic bed, with curtains fluttering and candles flickering all around. He had been thinking of me as he lay there.

"Listen—how did you know how to call me? Did you read about it in a book?"

"No," I said, thinking back. "I don't think so. I was just sitting here, miserable, and I thought if you were here, I'd feel better, and then this little rhyme came into my head, so I said it."

"Huh," Cal said thoughtfully.

"Was I not supposed to?" I asked, confused. "Sometimes things just come into my head like that."

"No, it's okay," said Cal. "It just means you're strong. You have ancestral memories of spells. Not every witch does." He nodded, thinking.

"So tell me more," he said. "Your parents never told you about this before, your being adopted?" He kept his arm on the back of the seat, smoothing my hair and rubbing my neck.

"No." I shook my head. "Never. And you'd think they would have—I'm so different from them."

Cal cocked his head, looking at me. "I've never met your folks," he said. "But you don't look much like your sister; that's true. Mary K. looks sweet." He smiled. "She's pretty."

A hot jealousy started to burn in my chest.

"You don't look sweet," Cal went on. "You look serious. Deep. Like you're thinking. And you're more striking than pretty. You're the kind of girl that you don't notice is beautiful until you get real close." His voice trailed off, and he brought his head closer to mine. "And then all of a sudden it hits you," he whispered. "And you think, Goddess, make her mine."

His lips touched mine again, and my thoughts whirled. I wrapped my arms around Cal's shoulders and kissed him as deeply as I knew how, pulling him closer. All I wanted was to be with him, to never be apart.

Minutes passed in which I heard only our breathing, our lips coming together and parting, the crinkle of the vinyl seat as we moved to be closer. Soon Cal was lying on top of me, his weight pressing me into the seat. His hand was stroking up and down my side, along my ribs and curving around my hip. Then it was under the hem of my jersey, warm against my breast, and shock waves went through me.

"Stop!" I said, almost afraid. "Wait."

My voice seemed to echo in the quiet car. Instantly Cal pulled his hand away. He held himself up, looking into my eyes, then leaned back against the driver's door. He was breathing fast.

I was mortified. You idiot, I thought. He's almost eighteen! He's definitely had sex. Maybe even with Bree, a tiny voice added.

I shook my head. "Sorry," I said, trying to sound casual. "It was just a surprise."

"No, no, *I'm* sorry," he said. He reached out and took my hand, and I was mesmerized by its warmth, its strength. "You call me here, and I jump on you. I shouldn't have. I'm sorry." He raised my fingers to his mouth and kissed them. "The thing is, I've been wanting to kiss you ever since I met you." He smiled slightly.

I calmed down. "I've wanted to kiss you, too," I admitted.

He smiled. "My witch," he said, running a finger down my cheek, leaving a thin trail of heat. "Now, how did you tell your mother that you're a blood witch?"

I sighed. "This morning she found a pile of my Wicca books, magick books, on the front porch. She stormed into my room, yelling at me, saying they were blasphemous." I sounded more together than I felt, remembering that awful scene. "I thought she was being so hypocritical—I mean, if I'm a blood witch, then she and my dad would have to be, too. Right?"

"Pretty much," said Cal. "Definitely, with someone who has powers as strong as yours, both your parents would have to be."

I frowned. "What about only one parent?"

"An ordinary man and a female witch can't conceive a baby," Cal explained. "A male witch can get an ordinary woman pregnant, but it's a conscious thing. And their baby would have very weak powers at best, or possibly none at all. Not like you."

I felt like I had accomplished something: I was a powerful witch.

"Okay," Cal said. "Now, why were your books on the front porch? Were you hiding them?"

"Yes," I said bitterly. "At Bree's house. This morning she

left them on my porch. Because you and I kissed last night."

"What?" Cal asked, a dark expression crossing his face.

I shrugged. "Bree really . . . wanted you. Wants you. And when you kissed me last night, I know she felt that I had betrayed her." I swallowed and looked out the window. "I *did* betray her," I said quietly. "I knew how she felt about you."

Cal's eyes dropped. He picked up a long strand of my hair and twined it around his hand, over and over. "How do *you* feel about me?" he asked after a moment.

Last night he had told me he loved me. I looked at him, seeing past him to the thin November sunlight that was burning away the fog. I breathed deeply, trying to slow the sudden, rapid patter of my pulse. "I love you," I said. My voice came out a husky whisper.

Cal glanced up and caught my gaze. His eyes were very bright. "I love you, too. I'm sorry that Bree's hurt, but just because she has feelings for me doesn't mean we're going to be together."

Did that stop you from sleeping with her? I almost asked him, but I couldn't quite bring myself to. I wasn't sure I really wanted to know.

"And I'm sorry Bree is taking it out on you," he said. He paused. "So your mom found the books and yelled. You thought she was hiding being a witch herself, right?"

"Yes. Not just her but my father and my sister," I said. "But my parents went crazy when I said that. I've never seen them so upset. And I said, so, what? I'm *adopted*? And they got these horrible expressions on their faces. They wouldn't answer me. And suddenly I had to know. So I ran downstairs and looked at my birth certificate."

"And there was a different name."

"Yeah. Maeve Riordan."

Cal sat up straighter, alert. "Really?"

I stared at him. "What? Do you recognize that name?"

"It sounds familiar." He looked out the window, thinking, frowning, then shook his head. "No, maybe not. I can't place it."

"Oh." I swallowed my disappointment.

"What are you going to do now? Do you want to come to my house?" He smiled. "We could go swimming."

"No, thank you," I said, remembering when the circle had all gone skinny-dipping in his pool. I was the only one who had kept her clothes on.

Cal laughed. "I was disappointed that night, you know," he said, looking at me.

"No, you weren't," I replied, crossing my arms over my chest. He chuckled softly.

"Seriously, do you want to come over? Or do you want me to come to your house, help you talk to your parents?"

"Thanks," I said, touched by his offer. "But I think I should just go home by myself. With any luck, they all went to church, anyway. It's All Saints' Day."

"What's that?" Cal asked.

I remembered he wasn't Catholic—wasn't even Christian. "All Saints' Day," I said. "It's the day after Halloween. It's a special day of observance for Catholics. That's when we go tend our family graves in cemeteries. Trim the grass, put out fresh flowers."

"Cool," said Cal. "That's a nice tradition. It's funny that it's the day after Samhain. But then, it seems like a lot of Christian holidays came out of Wiccan ones, way back when."

I nodded. "I know. But do me a favor and don't mention

that to my parents," I said. "Anyway, I'd better get home."

"Okay. Can I call you later?"

"Yes," I said. I couldn't stop myself from smiling.

"I think I'll use the telephone," he said, grinning.

I thought of how he had come when I had said my rhyme. I was still amazed that it had worked.

He let himself out of Das Boot into the chilly, crisp November air. He walked to his car and took off as I waved.

My world was flooded with sunlight. Cal loved me.

# 4

# Maeve

February 7, 1978

Two nights ago someone sprayed "Bloody Witch" on the side of Morag Sheehan's shop. We've moved our circle to meeting out by the cliffs, down the coast a ways.

Last night, late, Mathair and I went out to Morag's. Lucky it was a new moon — no light and a good time for spells.

### Rite of Healing, Protection from Evil, Cleansing

1. Cast a circle completely around what you want to protect. (I had to include old Burdock's sweetshop since the two buildings are joined.)

2. Purify the circle with salt. We used no lights or incense but salt, water, and earth.

3. Call on the Goddess. I wore my copper bracelets and held a chunk of sulfur, a chunk of marble from the garden, a chunk of petrified wood, and a bit of shell.

Then Ma and I said (quietly): "Goddess, hear us where we stand, with your protection bless this land, Morag is a servant true, protect her from those who mischief do." Then we invoked the Goddess and the God and walked around the shop three times.

No one saw us, that I could tell. Ma and I went home, feeling strong. That should help protect Morag. — Bradhadair

I drove slowly up my street, looking ahead anxiously as if my parents might still be standing on the front lawn of our house. When I was close enough, I saw that Dad's car was gone. I figured that they must have gone to church.

Inside, the house was quiet and still, though I felt the shocked vibrations of this morning's events lingering in the air like a scent.

"Mom? Dad? Mary K.?" I called. No answer. I wandered slowly through the house, seeing breakfast untouched on the kitchen table. I turned off the coffeemaker. The newspaper was folded neatly, obviously unread. Not at all a normal Sunday morning.

Realizing this was my chance, I hurried to the office. But the torn birth certificate was gone, and my dad's files were locked for the first time that I could remember.

Moving quickly, listening for sounds of their return, I searched the rest of the office. I found nothing and sat back on my heels for a moment, thinking.

My parents' room. I ran upstairs to their cluttered room. Feeling like a thief, I opened the top drawer of their dresser. Jewelry, cuff links, pens, bookmarks, old birthday cards—nothing incriminating, nothing that told me anything I needed to know.

Tapping my lip with my finger, I looked around. Framed baby pictures of me and Mary K. stood on top of their dresser, and I examined them. In one, my parents held me proudly, fat, nine-month-old Morgan, while I smiled and clapped. In another, Mom, in a hospital bed, held newborn Mary K., who looked like a hairless monkey. It occurred to me that I had never seen a newborn picture of me. Not a single one in the hospital, or looking tiny, or learning to sit up. My pictures started when I was about, what, eight months old? Nine months? Was that how old I was when I had been adopted?

Adopted. It was still such a bizarre thought, yet I was already eerily used to it. It explained everything, in a way. But in another way, it didn't. It only raised more questions.

I looked through my baby book, compared it to Mary K.'s. Mine listed my birth weight correctly and my birth date. Under First Impressions, Mom had written: "She's so incredibly beautiful. Everything I ever hoped for and dreamed about for so long."

I closed the book. How could they have lied to me all this time? How could they have let me believe I was really their daughter? I felt unstable now, without a base. Everything I had believed now seemed like a lie. How could I ever forgive them?

They had to give me some answers. I had the right to know. I dropped my head into my hands, feeling tired, old, and emotionally empty.

It was noon. Would they all have lunch at the Widow's Diner after church? Would they go on to the cemetery afterward to put flowers around the Rowlandses' graves and the Donovans', my mom's family?

Maybe they would. They probably would. I headed back into the kitchen, thinking that I should have some lunch myself. I hadn't eaten anything. But I was too upset to face food yet. Instead I took a Diet Coke out of the fridge. Then I found myself wandering into the study, where the computer was.

I decided to run a search. I frowned at the screen. How had her name been spelled, exactly? Maive? Mave? Maeve? The last name was Riordan, I remembered that.

I typed in Maeve Riordan. Twenty-seven listings popped up. Sighing, I started to scroll through them. A horse farm in western Massachusetts. A doctor in Dublin, specializing in ear problems. One by one I flipped through them, reading a few lines and closing their windows. I didn't know when my family would be home or what I would face when they arrived. My emotions felt flayed and yet distant, as if this were all happening to someone else.

Click. Maeve Riordan. Best-selling romance author presents *My Highland Love*.

Click. "Maeve Riordan" as part of an html. Frowning, I clicked on the link. This was a genealogy site, with links to other genealogy sites. Cool. It looked like the name Maeve Riordan appeared on three sites. I clicked on the first one. A scanty family tree popped up, and after a few minutes I found the name Maeve Riordan. Unfortunately, this Maeve Riordan had died in 1874.

I backtracked, and the next Maeve link took me to a site where there were no dates anywhere, as if they were still filling it in. I gritted my teeth in frustration.

Third time lucky, I thought, and clicked on the last site. The words *Belwicket and Ballynigel* appeared at the top of the screen in fancy Irish-style lettering. This was another family tree but with many separate branches, as if it was more of a family forest or the people hadn't found the common link between these families.

Quickly I scanned for Maeve Riordan. There were lots of Riordans. Then I saw it. *Maeve Riordan. Born Imbolc, 1962, Ballynigel, Ireland. Died Litha, 1986, Meshomah Falls, New York, United States.*

My jaw dropped open as I stared at the screen. Imbolc. Litha. Those were Wiccan sabbats. This Maeve Riordan had been a witch.

A sudden wave of heat pulsed through my head, making my cheeks prickle. I shook my head and tried to think. 1986. She died the year after I was born. And she was born in 1962. Which would have made her the same age as the woman listed on my birth certificate.

It's her, I thought. It has to be.

I clicked all over the screen, trying to find links. I felt almost frantic. I needed more information. More. But instead a message popped up: *Connection timed out. URL not responding.*

Frustrated, I shut down the computer. Then I sat tapping my lower lip with a pen. Thoughts raced through my head. Meshomah Falls, New York. I knew that name. It was a little town not too far away from here, maybe two hours. I needed to see their town records. I needed to see their . . . newspapers.

Two minutes later I had grabbed my jacket and was in Das Boot, heading for the library. Of Widow's Vale's three library branches, only the biggest one, downtown, was open on Sundays. I pushed through the glass door and immediately headed downstairs to the basement.

No one else was down there. The basement was empty except for rows and rows of books, out-of-date periodicals, stacks of books to be mended, and four ugly black-and-wood-grain microfiche machines.

Come on, come on, I thought, pawing through the microfiche files. It took twenty minutes to find the drawer containing past issues of the *Meshomah Falls Herald*. Another tedious fifteen minutes trying to figure dates, counting forward from my birthday to about eight months after it. Finally I pulled out an envelope, turned on a microfiche machine, and sat down.

I slid the tiny film card under the light and began to turn the knob.

Forty-five minutes later I rubbed the back of my neck. I now knew more about Meshomah Falls, New York, than anyone could possibly want to know. It was a farming community, smaller and even more boring than Widow's Vale.

I hadn't found anything about Maeve Riordan. No obituary, nothing. Well, that wasn't really surprising. I should probably get used to the idea that I would never know about my past.

There were two more film cards to look at. With a sigh I sat down again, hating the machine.

This time I found the article almost immediately. The little hairs on the back of my neck prickled, and there it was: Maeve Riordan. Stiffening in my chair, I scrolled back to center the page and peered into the viewer. *A body burned almost beyond recognition has been identified as that of Maeve Riordan, formerly of Ballynigel, Ireland....*

My breath caught in my throat, and I stared at the screen. Was this her? I wondered again. My birth mother? I'd never been to Meshomah Falls. I'd never heard my parents talk about it. But Maeve Riordan had lived there. And somehow, in Meshomah Falls, Maeve Riordan had died in a fire.

I surprised myself by shaking uncontrollably as I gazed blankly at the screen. Quickly I scanned the short news clipping.

On June 21, 1986, the body of an unidentified young woman had been found in the ruins of a charred and smoldering barn on an abandoned farm in Meshomah Falls. After an examination of dental X-rays, the body had been identified as belonging to one Maeve Riordan, who had been renting a small house in Meshomah Falls and working at the local café downtown. Maeve Riordan, twenty-three years old, formerly of Ballynigel, Ireland, was not well known in the town. Another body found in the fire had been identified as Angus Bramson, twenty-five years old, also of Ballynigel. It was unknown why they were in the barn. The cause of the fire seemed unclear.

June 21 might have been Litha in that year—it varied according to exactly when the equinox was. But what about a baby? It didn't say anything about a baby.

My heart was thudding painfully inside my chest. Images of a recent dream I'd had, of being in a rough sort of room while a woman held me and called me her baby, flashed through my head. What did this all mean?

Abruptly I shut off the machine. I stood up so fast, I felt dizzy and had to clutch the back of my chair.

I was almost certain that this Maeve Riordan had given birth to me. Why had she given me up for adoption? Or was I only adopted after she died? Was Angus Bramson my father? How had that barn caught on fire?

Moving slowly, I put all the microfiche files where I had found them. Then, my hands to my temples, I went upstairs and walked out of the library. Outside it was gray and overcast, and the library's lawn was covered with bright yellow maple leaves. It was autumn, and winter was on the way.

The seasons changed with such a gradual grace, easing you gently from one to the next. But my life, my whole life, had changed in a bare moment.

# 5

# Reasons

Samhain, October 31, 1978

Ma and Da just went over this Book of Shadows and said it was a poor one indeed. I need to write more often; I need to explain spells more; I need to explain the workings of the moon, the sun, the tides, the stars. I said, Why? Everybody knows that stuff. Ma said it's for my children, the witches who come after me. Like how she and Da show me their books — they've got five of them now, those big thick black books by the fireplace. When I was little, I thought they were photo albums. It makes me laugh now — photos of witches.

But you know, my spells and stuff are in my head. There's time to put them down later. Plenty of time. Mostly I want to write about my feelings and thoughts. But then, I don't want my folks to read that — when they got to the parts when I was kissing Angus, they blew up! But they know Angus, and they like him. They see him often enough, know that I've settled on him. Angus is good, and who else is there for me here? It's not like I can be with just anyone, not if I want to live my life and have kids and all. Lucky for me Angus is as sweet as he is.

Here's a good spell for making love fade: During a waning moon, gather four hairs from a black cat, a cat that has no white anywhere on her. Take a white candle, the dried petals of three red roses, and a piece of string. Write your name and the name of the person you want to push away on two pieces of paper, and tie one to each end of the string.

Go outside. (This works best under a new moon or a moon the day before the new moon.) Set up your altar; purify your circle; invoke the Goddess. Set up your white candle. Sprinkle the rose petals around the candle. Take each of the cat's hairs and set them at the four points of the compass: N, S, E, and W. (Hold them down with rocks if the night's windy.) Light the candle and hold the middle of the string taut over the candle, about five inches up. Then say:

As the moon wanes, so wanes your love;
I am an eagle, no more your dove.
Another face, more fair than mine,
Will surely win your love in time.

Say that over and over until the string burns through and the two names are separated forever. Don't do this in anger because your love really will no more be yours. You have to want to truly get rid of someone forever.

P.S. The cat hairs don't do anything. I just put them in to sound mysterious.

— Bradhadair

I was in the kitchen, eating some warmed-up lasagna, when my parents and Mary K. came home late that afternoon. They all stared at me as if they had come home to find a stranger in their kitchen.

"Morgan," said my dad, clearing his throat. His eyes looked red-rimmed, his face drawn and older than this morning. His thinning black hair was brushed tightly against his scalp, too long on the ends. His thick, wire-rimmed glasses gave him an owlish look.

"Yes?" I said, marveling at the cold steadiness of my voice. I took a sip of soda.

"Are you all right?"

It was such a ludicrous question, but it was so like my dad to ask.

"Well, let's see," I said coolly, not looking at him. "I just found out I was adopted. I've been sitting here realizing you've both been lying to me my whole life." I shrugged. "Other than that, I'm fine."

Mary K. looked like she was about to burst into tears. In fact, she looked like she had been crying all morning.

"Morgan," said my mom. "Maybe we made the wrong decision in not telling you. But we had our reasons. We love you, and we're still your parents."

I couldn't stay cool any longer. "Your reasons?" I exclaimed. "You had good reasons for not telling me the most important fact of my life? There are no good reasons for that!"

"Morgan, stop," Mary K. said, her voice wobbling. "We're a family. I just want you to be my sister." She started crying, and I felt my own throat tighten.

"I want you to be my sister, too," I said, standing up. "But I don't know what's going on anymore—what's real and what's not."

Mary K. burst into real sobs and threw herself on Dad's shoulder.

Mom tried to come over to me, to take me in her arms, but I backed away. I couldn't stand her touch right at that second. She looked stricken.

"Look, let's not say anything right now," Dad said. "We need some time. We've all had a shock. Please, Morgan, just hear me on one thing: Your mother and I have two daughters whom we love more than anything in the world. Two daughters."

"Mary K. is your daughter," I said, hating hearing my voice crack. "Biologically. But I'm nobody!"

"Don't say that!" Mom said, looking devastated.

"You're both our daughters," said my dad. "And you always will be."

It was about the most comforting thing he could have said, and it made me burst into tears. I was so exhausted, physically and emotionally, that I stumbled upstairs to my room, lay on my bed, and began to drift toward sleep.

While I was half dreaming, half awake, my mom came into my room and sat on the bed next to me. She stroked my hair, her fingers gently working through the tangles. It reminded me of my dream, my other mother. Maybe it wasn't a dream, I thought. Maybe it was a memory.

"Mom," I said.

"Shhh, sweetie, sleep," she whispered. "I just wanted to say I love you, and I'm your mother, and you've been my daughter since the first second I laid eyes on you."

I shook my head, wanting to protest that it wasn't true, but I was already too close to sleep. As I drifted off into a deep, blessed numbness I was aware of warm tears soaking my pillow. I don't know if they were hers or mine.

The next morning was bizarre in how ordinary it seemed. As usual, Mom and Dad got up and went to work early, before I was even awake. As usual, Mary K. yelled for me to hurry as I drifted through my shower, trying to brace myself for the day.

Mary K. looked pale and pinch-faced and was unusually quiet as I gulped down a Diet Coke and threw books into my backpack.

"I want you to stop what you're doing," she said so softly, I could barely hear her. "I want us to go back to being how we were."

I sighed. I had never felt jealous or competitive when it came to Mary K. I'd always wanted to take care of her. I wondered if it would be different now. I had no idea. But I knew that I still hated seeing her hurt.

"It's too late for that," I said quietly. "And I need to know the truth. There have been too many secrets for too long."

Mary K. raised her hands, and they fluttered for a moment in midair as she tried to think of something to say. But there wasn't anything to say, and in the end we just got our backpacks and headed outside to Das Boot.

Cal was waiting for me at school. He walked over to my

car as I parked and met me as I opened the door. Mary K. looked at him, as if to measure his involvement in all of this. He met her gaze calmly, sympathetically.

"I'm Cal," he said, holding out his hand. "Cal Blaire. I don't think we've really met."

Mary K. looked at him. "I know who you are," she said, not taking his hand. "Are you doing witchcraft with Morgan?"

"Mary K.!" I started, but Cal held up his hand.

"It's okay," he said. "Yes, I'm doing witchcraft with Morgan. But we're not doing anything wrong."

"Wrong for who?" Mary K. sounded older than fourteen. She slid past Cal and got out of the car. She was immediately surrounded by her friends, but she looked unhappy and withdrawn. I wondered what she would tell them. Then Bakker Blackburn, her boyfriend, came up. They walked off together.

"How are you?" Cal asked, and kissed my forehead. "I've been thinking about you. I called last night, but your mom said you were asleep."

I saw people looking at us, Alessandra Spotford, Nell Norton, Justin Bartlett. Of course they were surprised to see Cal Blaire, human god, with Morgan Rowlands, Girl Most Likely to Remain Dateless Forever.

"Yeah—I think my brain just shut down. Thanks for calling. I'll tell you about everything later." He squeezed my shoulder, and together we walked up to where the coven— we were a coven now and not just a group of friends—hung out, on the cement benches by the east side of the school. The redbrick building looked reassuringly familiar and unchanged, but that was about the only thing in my life that was the same today.

Seven pairs of eyes were on us as we came up the crumbling brick walkway. I sought out Bree's face. She was studiously examining her brown suede boots. She looked beautiful and remote, cool and aloof. Two weeks ago she had been my best friend in the world, the person I loved most besides my family, the person who knew me the best.

Something in me still cared about her, still wanted to confide in her, as impossible as that was. I thought about telling my problems to one of my other friends, like Tamara Pritchett or Janice Yutoh, but I knew I couldn't.

"Hi, Morgan, Cal," said Jenna Ruiz, her face as open and friendly as ever. She gave me a sincere smile, and I smiled back. Matt Adler was sitting next to her, his arm around her shoulders. Jenna coughed, covering her mouth, and for a moment Matt looked at her in concern. She shook her head and smiled at him.

"Hi, Jenna. Everyone," I said.

Raven Meltzer was looking at me with open dislike. Her dark eyes, heavily rimmed with kohl and sprinkled with glitter, glowed with an inner anger. She had wanted Cal for herself, like Bree. Like me.

"Samhain was amazing," said Sharon Goodfine, crossing her arms over her ample chest as if she were cold. She gave the word its proper pronunciation: Sowen. "I feel so different. I felt different all weekend." Her carefully made-up face looked thoughtful rather than snobbish.

Without thinking about what I was doing, I cast my senses out, gently, carefully, feeling for the emotions of the people surrounding me. It was like what I'd experienced during the circle in the cemetery, but this time I directed it. This time I did it on purpose.

It occurred to me only in passing that perhaps my friends' emotions should be private, belonging only to them.

Jenna was just as she appeared; open, good-natured. Matt seemed the same, but deep within him I sensed a dark space he kept to himself. Cal . . . Cal glanced at me in quick surprise as my sense net touched his mind. As I scanned him I felt a sudden, hot rush of desire from him, and I blushed and pulled back quickly. He gave me a look, as if to say, Well, you asked. . . .

Ethan Sharp was interesting—a colorful mosaic of thoughts and feelings, tightly held distrust, poetry, and disappointment. Sharon had a stillness to her, a calm center that seemed new. There was also a hesitant, half-embarrassed tenderness—for whom? Ethan?

Beth Nielson, Raven's best friend, mainly seemed bored and wanted to be somewhere else. My best friend after Bree, Robbie Gurevitch, was startling: a mixture of anger, desire, and repressed emotion that didn't show at all on his face. Who was it directed at? I couldn't tell.

But it was Bree and Raven who almost blew me off the bench. Deep, intense waves of fury and jealousy came from both of them, aimed at me and, to a lesser extent, Cal. With Raven it was all jagged, snaggletoothed edges of anger and frustration and hunger. For all her reputation of being easy, she hadn't actually ever been linked seriously to anyone. Maybe she had wanted Cal to be the one.

If Raven's feelings were barbed wire, Bree's were smoldering coals. Instantly I knew that as much as she had loved me two weeks ago, she now hated me to the same extent. She had been desperate for Cal. Maybe it wasn't real love, but it was a powerful desire, that was certain. And she had never before wanted a guy without his wanting her back. Cal had deeply wounded her when he had chosen me over her.

All these impressions had taken only a moment. A heartbeat and the knowledge was within me.

It struck me that none of these people, the people in my coven, knew about my adoption, except Cal. It was such a huge, momentous thing, so life changing, so frightening, yet it had all happened in one day, yesterday. And yesterday had been just another Sunday for them. It made me feel disoriented and strange.

"So," Bree said, breaking the silence. She didn't look at me. "Did your parents enjoy their new reading material?"

I blinked. If only she knew what her revenge had begun. All I could do was shake my head and sit down. I didn't trust myself to talk.

Bree smirked, still gazing at her boots.

Cal took my hand in his, and I held it tightly.

"What are you talking about, Bree?" Robbie asked. He took off his thick glasses and rubbed his eyes. Without his glasses he looked like a different person. The spell I had performed two weeks before had worked better than I could have possibly imagined. His skin, once pitted with acne scars, now was smooth and fine textured, showing a dim outline of dark beard. His nose was straight and classical, where it had been swollen and red. Even his lips seemed firmer, more attractive, though I couldn't remember how they had been before.

"Nothing," Bree said lightly. "It's not important."

No, it was just the destruction of my life, I thought.

"Whatever," Robbie muttered, rubbing his eyes. "Damn. Anyone have some Tylenol? I have an incredible headache."

"I've got some," said Sharon, reaching for her purse.

"Always prepared," said Ethan with a smile. "Like a Girl Scout." Sharon shot him a look, then gave Robbie two pills, which he took dry.

Our coven had united cool kids with losers, brains and geeks and stoners and princesses. It was interesting to watch people who were so different from one another interact.

"I had a good time on Saturday night," Cal said after a pause. "I'm glad you all came. It was a good way to celebrate the most important Wiccan holiday."

"It was so cool," said Jenna. "And Morgan was amazing!"

I felt self-conscious and gave my knees a tiny smile.

"It was really awesome," said Matt. "I spent most of the day yesterday on the Web, looking up Wiccan sites. There's a million of them, and some of them are pretty intense."

Jenna laughed. "And some of them are so lame! Some of those people are so weird! And they have the cheesiest music."

"I like the ones with chat rooms," said Ethan. "If you get one where people know what they're talking about, it's really interesting. Sometimes they have spells and stuff to download."

"There's a lot about Yule coming up in a couple of months," said Sharon.

"Maybe we could have a Yule party," I said, caught up in their talk. Then I saw the looks that Raven and Bree were giving me: superior, snide looks as if I were an annoying little sister instead of the most talented student in our coven. My jaw set, and at that instant I saw a large, curled maple leaf that was drifting lazily earthward. Without thinking, I caught it with my mind and sent it floating over Raven's head.

I kept my gaze on it, holding it in place while it hovered over her shiny black hair. Then it rested, ever so lightly, on her head, and it became a ludicrous, laughable hat.

I laughed openly, pleased with myself, and Raven's eyes narrowed, not understanding. She couldn't feel the large leaf perching there like a flat brown pancake, but it looked absurd.

Jenna saw it next, then our whole coven was looking at Raven and grinning, except Cal.

"What?" Raven snapped. "What are you looking at?"

Even Bree had to bite back a smile as she swept the leaf off Raven's head. "It was just a leaf," she said.

Flustered, Raven picked up her black bag just as the homeroom bell rang.

We all got up to go to class. I was still smiling when Cal leaned over me and whispered, "Remember the threefold law." He touched my cheek softly and then left, heading toward the other school entrance for his first class.

I swallowed. The Wiccan threefold law was one of the most important tenets of the craft. Basically it stated that anything you sowed, good or evil, would come back to you threefold, so always put good out there. Don't put bad. Cal was telling me (1) he knew I had controlled the leaf, and (2) he knew I was being mean when I did it. And it wasn't cool.

Taking a deep breath, I pulled my backpack strap over my shoulder.

As soon as Cal was out of earshot, Raven said nastily, "Okay, so he's yours—for now. But how long do you think that's going to last?"

"Yeah," Bree murmured. "Wait till he finds out you're a virgin. He'll find that pretty amusing."

My cheeks flamed. I had a sudden image of his hand under my shirt yesterday morning and how I had jumped.

Raven raised her eyebrows. "Don't tell me she's a virgin?"

"Oh, Raven, leave it," Beth said, brushing past her. Raven watched her for a second in surprise, then turned her attention back to me.

Bree and Raven laughed together, and I stared at Bree. How could she reveal such a personal thing about me? I kept my mouth stonily shut and kept walking to home-room—which I shared with Bree, of course.

"Come on, Raven," said Bree, behind me. "Anyone looking at her can tell *that* isn't why he wants her."

I couldn't believe it. Bree, who had always told me I was too negative about my looks, who insisted my flat chest didn't matter, who had worked for years to get me to see myself as attractive. She was turning on me so completely.

"You know what it is, don't you?" Raven sniped on. Did either of them have any clue that I was ready to kill them both? I wondered. "Cal saw her, and it was witch at first sight."

I ran to class, hearing the echoes of their laughter floating behind me. Those *bitches,* I snarled to myself. In class I sat for ten minutes, trying to calm my breathing, trying to release my anger.

For just a moment I was glad I had been mean to Raven. I should have been ten times as mean. I couldn't help it. I wanted to wipe Bree and Raven out. I wanted to see them miserable.

# 6

# Searching

January 9, 1980

They found Morag Sheehan's body last evening. Down at the bottom of the cliffs, by old Towson's farm. The tide would have taken her away and none of us the wiser, but it was a low tide because of the moon. And so she was found by young Billy Martin and Hugh Beecham. At first they thought she was the charred, rotted mast of a ship. But she wasn't. She was only a burned witch.

Of course Belwicket met before dawn. We hung blankets over the shutters inside and gathered around my folks' kitchen table. The thing is, Ma and I had put that powerful protection on Morag last year, and since then nothing had gone amiss with her. All was right as rain.

"You know what this means," said Paddy McTavish. "No human could have got close to her, not with that spell on her and all the ward-evil spells she was doing herself."

"What are you saying?" Ma asked.

"I'm saying she was killed by a witch," Paddy answered.

When he said that, of course it seemed obvious. Morag was killed by a witch. One of us? Surely not. Then is there someone in the neighborhood, someone we don't know about? Someone from a different coven?

It makes me cold to think of such evil.

Next circle we're going to scry. Until then I'm keeping a weather eye on everybody and everything. — Bradhadair

The first chance I had to tell Cal about my research was after school. He walked with me to Das Boot, and we stood by my car and talked. "I found out about Maeve Riordan," I said bluntly. "A little bit, anyway."

"Tell me about it," he said, but I saw him glance at his watch.

"Do you need to go?" I asked.

"In a minute," he said apologetically. "My mom needs me to help her this afternoon. One of her coven members is sick, and we're going to do some healing."

"You can do that?" It seemed every day I learned of new magickal possibilities.

"Sure," Cal said. "I'm not saying we'll definitely cure him, but he'll do a lot better than if we weren't working for him. But tell me what you found out."

"I ran a search on the computer," I said. "I hit a lot of dead ends. But I found her name on a genealogy site, which led me to a small article from the *Meshomah Falls Herald*. So I looked it up at the library."

"Where's Meshomah Falls?" asked Cal.

"Just a few hours from here. Anyway, the article said that a burned body had been identified as Maeve Riordan, formerly of Ballynigel, Ireland. She was twenty-three."

Cal wrinkled his brow. "Do you think that's her?" he asked.

I nodded. "I think it must be. I mean, there were other Maeve Riordans. But this one was close to here, and the timing's right. . . . When she died, I would have been about seven months old."

"Did the article mention a baby?" asked Cal.

I shook my head.

"Huh." He stroked my hair. "I wonder if there's somewhere else we could get more information. Let me think about it. Will you be okay? I don't want to leave, but I kind of have to."

"I'm okay," I said, looking up into his face, relishing the fact that he cared about me. And it wasn't just because I was a blood witch like him. Raven and Bree were just jealous—they didn't know what they were talking about.

We kissed gently, then Cal headed toward his car. I watched him drive off.

Motion caught my eye, and I glanced over to see Tamara and Janice about to get into Tamara's car. They grinned at me and raised their eyebrows suggestively. Tamara gave me a thumbs-up. I grinned back, embarrassed but pleased. As they drove off, it occurred to me that the three of us should try to see a movie soon.

"Skipping chess club?" came Robbie's voice.

I blinked and looked around to see Robbie loping toward me, sunlight flashing from his glasses. His choppy brown hair that only last month had looked so awful now seemed to have a rakish trendiness.

I considered for a moment. "Yeah, I am," I said. "I don't know—chess seems kind of pointless now."

"Not chess itself," Robbie said, his blue-gray eyes serious behind his ugly glasses. "Chess itself is still really awesome. It's beautiful, like a crystal."

I braced myself for one of Robbie's chess rants. He's almost in love with the game. But he just said, "It's just the club thing that's pointless now. The school thing." He looked at me. "After you've seen a friend of yours make a flower bloom, school and clubs and all of that seem kind of . . . silly."

I felt proud and self-conscious at the same time. I loved the idea that I was gifted, that my heritage was showing in my ability. But I was also so used to blending in with the woodwork, not making waves, standing happily in Bree's shadow. It was hard to get used to being noticed so much.

"Are you going home?" Robbie asked.

"I don't know. I don't really feel like it," I said. In fact, the thought of facing my parents made my stomach knot up. Then I had a better idea. "Hey, do you want to go to Practical Magick?" I felt a mixture of guilt and pleasure as I suggested it. My mom definitely wouldn't approve of my going to a Wicca store. But so what? It wasn't my problem.

"Cool," said Robbie. "Then we'll hit Baskin-Robbins. Leave your car here, and I'll bring you back to it."

"Let's do it." As I was walking up the street to Robbie's car, I caught a flash of Mary K.'s straight auburn hair. Glancing over, my eyes locked on Mary K. and Bakker plastered together against the side of the life sciences building. My eyes narrowed. It was the most bizarre feeling, seeing my four-teen-year-old sister making out with someone.

"Go, Bakker," Robbie murmured, and I punched his arm.

I couldn't help looking at them as we approached Robbie's dark red VW Beetle. I saw Mary K., laughing, squirming out of Bakker's arms. He followed her and caught her again.

"Bakker!" Mary K. squealed, her hair flying.

"Mary K.!" I called suddenly, without knowing why.

She looked up, still caught in his arms. "Hey."

"I'm getting a ride with Robbie," I said, gesturing to him.

Nodding, she motioned toward Bakker. "Bakker will take me home. Right?" she asked him.

He nuzzled her neck. "Whatever you say."

Suppressing a feeling of unease, I got into Robbie's car.

The drive north to Red Kill took only about twenty-five minutes. After Das Boot, Robbie's car felt small and intimate. I noticed Robbie squinting and rubbing his eyes.

"You've been doing that a lot lately," I said.

"My eyes are killing me. I need new glasses," he said. "My mom made an appointment for tomorrow."

"Good."

"What was Bree talking about this morning?" he asked. "About your parents' new reading material?"

I wrinkled my nose and sighed. "Well, Bree is really angry at me," I said, stating the obvious. "It's all about Cal—she wanted to go out with him, and he wanted to go out with me. So now she hates me, I guess. Anyway—you know I was keeping my Wicca books at her house?"

Robbie nodded, his eyes on the road.

"She dumped them all on my porch yesterday morning," I explained. "My mom went ballistic. It's all a big mess," I summed up inadequately.

"Oh," said Robbie.

"Yeah."

"I knew Bree liked Cal," said Robbie. "I didn't think they would be a good couple."

I smiled at him, amused. "Bree would make anyone into a good couple. Anyway, let's not talk about it. Things have been kind of . . . awful. The only good thing is that Cal and I got together, and it's really great."

Robbie glanced over at me and nodded. "Hmmm," he said.

"Hmmm, what?" I asked. "Do you mean, hmmm, that's great? Or hmmm, I'm not so sure?"

"More like—hmmm, it's complicated, I guess," Robbie told me. "You know, because of Bree and everything."

I stared at him, but he was watching the road again, and I couldn't read his profile.

I looked out the window. I wanted to talk about something that we hadn't really hashed out. "Robbie, I really am sorry about that spell. You know. The one about your skin."

He shifted gears without saying anything.

"I won't ever do it again," I promised once more.

"Don't say that. Just promise you won't do it without telling me," he said as he parked his Beetle in a tiny space. He turned to me. "I was mad that you did it without telling me," he said. "But I mean, Jesus, look at me." He gestured to his newly smooth face. "I never thought I'd look like this. Thought I'd be a pizza face forever. Then have awful scars my whole life." He glanced out over the steering wheel. "Now I look in the mirror and I'm happy. Girls look at me—girls who used to ignore me or feel sorry for me." He shrugged. "How could I be upset about that?"

I reached out and touched his arm. "Thanks."

He grinned at me and swung open his door. "Let's go get in touch with our inner witches."

As usual, Practical Magick was dim and scented with herbs, oils, and incense. After the chilly November sunshine, the store felt warm and welcoming. Inside, it was divided in two, one half floor-to-ceiling bookshelves and the other half shelves covered with candles, herbs, essential oils, altar items and magical symbols, ritual daggers called athames, robes, posters, even Wiccan fridge magnets.

I left Robbie looking at books and went over to the herb section. Learning about working with them could take my whole life and then some, I thought. The idea was daunting but also thrilling. I had used herbs in the spell that had cured Robbie's acne, and I had felt almost transported in the herb garden of the Killburn Abbey, when I'd gone there on a church trip.

I was looking through a guide to magickal plants of the northeast when I felt a tingling sensation. Glancing up, I saw David, one of the store's clerks. I tensed. He always put me on edge, and I could never pinpoint why.

I remembered how he had asked me what clan I was in and how he had told Alyce, the other clerk, that I was a witch who pretended not to be a witch.

Now I watched him warily as he walked toward me, his short, gray hair looking silver in the store's fluorescent lights.

"Something about you has changed," he said in his soft voice, his brown eyes on me.

I thought about Samhain, when the night had exploded

around me, and about Sunday, when my family had blown apart. I didn't say anything.

"You're a blood witch," he stated, nodding as if he were simply confirming something I'd said. "And now you know it."

How can he tell? I wondered with a tinge of fear.

"Were you really surprised?" he asked me.

I looked around for Robbie. He was still over by the books.

"Yes, I was kind of surprised," I admitted.

"Do you have your BOS?" he asked. "Book of Shadows?"

"I've started one," I said, thinking of the beautiful blank book with marbled paper that I had bought a couple of weeks before. In it I had written down the spell I had done for Robbie and also about my experiences on Samhain. But why did David want to know?

"Do you have your clan's, your coven's?" he asked. "Your mother's?"

"No," I said shortly. "No chance of that."

"I'm sorry," he said, after a pause. Then a bell tinkled, and he moved off to help another customer choose some jewelry.

Glancing down the aisle, I saw that the other clerk, Alyce, was on the floor way at the end, arranging some candleholders on a low shelf. She was older than David, a round, motherly woman with beautiful gray hair in a loose bun on top of her head. I had liked her the first moment I had seen her. Still holding my herb book, I wandered down the aisle closer to her.

She looked up and smiled briefly, as if she had been waiting for me. "How are you, dear?" There was a world of meaning in her words, and for a moment I felt like she knew about everything that had happened since she had helped me pick out a candle, a week before Samhain.

I didn't know what to say. "Awful," I blurted out. "I just found out I'm a blood witch. My parents have lied to me all my life."

Alyce nodded knowingly. "So David was right," she said, her voice reaching me alone. "I thought you were, too."

"How did you know?"

"We can recognize them," she said matter-of-factly. "We're blood witches ourselves, though we don't know our clans."

I stared at her.

"David in particular is quite powerful," Alyce went on. Her plump hands made neat rows of candleholders shaped like stars, like moons, like pentacles.

"Do you have a coven?" I whispered.

"Starlocket," said Alyce. "With Selene Belltower."

Cal's mother.

Robbie appeared at the end of the aisle, thirty feet away. He was talking to a young woman, who was smiling at him flirtatiously. Robbie pushed his glasses aside, rubbed his eyes, then answered her. She laughed, and they drifted back over to the book aisle. I heard the murmur of their voices. For a moment curiosity made me want to concentrate on hearing their words, but then I realized that just because I could didn't mean I should.

A sudden idea sparked in my head. "Alyce, do you know anything about Meshomah Falls?" I asked.

It was as if a snake had bitten her. She literally drew back, anguish crossing her round face. Frowning, she got slowly to her feet, as if troubled by a great weight.

She looked into my eyes. "Why do you ask?" she said.

"I wanted to know more about . . . a woman named Maeve Riordan," I said. "I need to know more."

For long moments Alyce's gaze held mine.

"I know that name," she said.

# 7

# Burned

May 8, 1980

Angus asked me to marry him at Beltane. I told him no. I'm only eighteen and have hardly ever been out of Ballynigel. I was thinking of doing one of those tours, you know, with a bus and going through Europe for a month. I do love Angus. And I know he's good. He might even be my mùirn beatha dàn, my soul mate, but who knows? He might not! Sometimes I feel like he is, sometimes I don't. The thing is: How would I know? I've met precious few witches in my life that I'm not related to. I need to be sure. I need to know more before I can decide to stay with him forever.

"Where will you go?" he asks me. "Who will you be with? Someone not your kind, like David O'Hearn? A human?"

Of course not. If I want children, I can't be with a human. But maybe I don't want children. I don't know. There aren't that many of our clan. To go outside our clan to another would be disloyal. But to seal my fate at eighteen seems disloyal, too — disloyal to me.

*And after all that's been happening — Morag's murder, the bad-luck spells, the bespelled runes (Mathair calls them sigils) we've found — I just don't know. I want to get away. Only three more weeks and I'll take my A levels and be done with school. I can't wait.*

*Now it's late, and I have to do a warding spell before I sleep, to keep away evil. We all do, nowadays. — Bradhadair*

I waited while Alyce cast back her mind. There was a tall stool nearby, battered and blotched with multicolored paint spills. I perched on it, my eyes on Alyce's face.

"I never knew Maeve Riordan," Alyce said at last. "I never met her. I was living in Manhattan at the time all of this happened. I really only learned of it years later, when I moved here. But it was big news in the Wiccan community, and most witches around here know about it."

It was shocking to me that many people knew the story of what had happened to my mother while I knew virtually nothing. I waited, not wanting to disturb Alyce's thoughts.

"The way I heard the story is this," Alyce said, and it was as if her voice were coming to me from a distance. "Maeve Riordan was a blood witch, from one of the Seven Great Clans, but we aren't sure which one. Her local coven was called Belwicket, and she was from Ballynigel, Ireland."

I nodded. I had seen the words Belwicket and Ballynigel on Maeve's genealogy site, the one that had shut down.

"Belwicket was very insular and didn't interact with other clans or covens much," Alyce continued. "They were quite secretive, and maybe they had cause to be. Anyway, back in the late seventies, early eighties, as I understand it, Belwicket was persecuted. The members were taunted in the streets by the townspeople; their children were ostracized at school. Ballynigel was a small town, mind you, small and close to the coast of western Ireland. The people there were mainly farmers or fishermen. Not worldly, not overly educated. Very conservative," Alyce explained. She paused, thinking.

In my mind I saw rolling hills as deep a green as a peridot. Salt air seemed to kiss my skin. I smelled tangy, brackish seaweed, fish, and an almost unpleasant yet comfortable odor my brain identified as peat, whatever that was.

"The villagers had probably always lived among witches in peace, but for some reason, every so often, a town gets stirred up; people get scared. After months of persecution a local witch was murdered, burned to death and thrown from a cliff."

I swallowed hard. I knew from my reading that burning was the traditional method of killing witches.

"There was some talk that it had been another witch, not a human, who had done it," continued Alyce.

"What about Maeve Riordan?" I asked.

"She was the daughter of the local high priestess, a woman named Mackenna Riordan. At fourteen Maeve joined Belwicket under the name Bradhadair: fire starter. Apparently she was very powerful, very, very powerful."

My mother.

"Anyway, things in Ballynigel grew more and more intolerable for the witches. They had to shop in other towns, leases expired and weren't renewed, but they could deal with all that somehow."

"Why didn't they leave?" I asked.

"Ballynigel was a place of power," Alyce explained. "At least it was for that coven. There was something about that area, perhaps just because magick had been worked there for centuries—but it was a very good place to be for a witch. Most of Belwicket had roots in the land going back more generations than they could count. Their people had always lived there. I imagine it was hard to fathom living anywhere else."

It was hard for an American, with family roots going back only a hundred years or so, to comprehend. Taking a deep breath, I looked around for Robbie. I could hear him still talking to the girl on the other side of the store. I glanced at my watch. Five-thirty. I had to get home soon. But I was finally learning about my past, my history, and I couldn't pull myself away.

"How do you know all this?" I asked.

"People have talked of it over the years," Alyce said. "You see, it could so easily happen to any of us."

A chill went through me, and I stared at her. To me, magick was beautiful and joyful. She was reminding me that countless women and men had died because of it.

"Maeve Riordan finally did leave," Alyce went on, her face sad. "One night there was a huge . . . decimation, for want of a better word."

I shivered, feeling an icy breeze float over me, settling at my feet.

"The Belwicket coven was virtually destroyed," Alyce continued, sounding like the words were hard to say. "It's unclear whether it was the townspeople or a dark, powerful, magickal source that swept through the coven, but that night homes were burned to the ground, cars were set on fire, fields of crops were laid to waste, boats were sunk . . . and twenty-three men, women, and children were killed."

I realized I was panting, my stomach in knots. I felt ill and dizzy and panicky. I couldn't bear hearing about this.

"But not Maeve," Alyce whispered, looking off at some far-away sight. "Maeve escaped that night, and so did young Angus Bramson, her lover. Maeve was twenty, Angus twenty-two, and together they fled, caught a bus to Dublin and a plane to England. From there they landed in New York, and from New York City they made their way to Meshomah Falls."

"Did they get married?" I said hoarsely.

"There's no record of it," Alyce replied. "They settled in Meshomah Falls, got jobs, and renounced witchcraft entirely. Apparently for two years they practiced no Wicca, called upon no power, created no magick." She shook her head sadly. "It must have been like living in a straitjacket. Like smothering inside a box. And then they had a baby in the local hospital. We think the persecution began right after that."

My throat felt like it was closing. I pulled my sweater away from my neck because it was choking me.

"It was little things at first—finding runes of danger and threat painted on the side of their little house. Evil sigils, runes bespelled for some magickal purpose, scratched into their car doors. One day a dead cat hanging from their porch. If they had come to the local coven, they could have been helped. But they wanted nothing to do with witchcraft. After Belwicket had been destroyed, Maeve wanted nothing more to do with it. Though, of course, it was in her blood. There's no point in denying what you are."

Terror threatened to overwhelm me. I wanted to run screaming from the store.

Alyce looked at me. "Maeve's Book of Shadows was found after the fire. People read it and passed on the stories of what was written there."

"Where is it now?" I demanded, and Alyce shook her head.

"I don't know," she said gently. "Maeve's story ends with her and Angus burned in a barn."

Tears ran slowly down my cheeks.

"What happened to the baby?" I choked out.

Alyce gazed at me sympathetically, years of wisdom written on her face. She reached up one soft, flower-scented hand and touched my cheek. "I don't know that, either, my dear," she said so quietly, I could barely hear her. "What did happen to the baby?"

A mist swam over my eyes, and I needed to lie down or fall over or run screaming down the street.

"Hey, Morgan!" Robbie's voice broke in. "Are you ready? I should get home."

"Good-bye," I whispered. I turned and raced out the door, with Robbie following me, concern radiating from him in waves.

Behind me I felt rather than heard Alyce's words: "Not good-bye, my dear. You'll be back."

# 8
# Anger

November 1, 1980

What a glorious Samhain we had last night! After a powerful circle that Ma let me lead, we danced, played music, watched the stars, and hoped for better times ahead. It was a night full of cider, laughter, and hope. Things have been so quiet lately — has the evil moved on? Has it found another home? Goddess, I pray not, for I don't wish others to suffer as we have. But I'm thankful that we no longer have to jump at every noise.

Angus gave me a darling kitten — a tiny white tom I've named Dagda. He has a lot to live up to with that name! He's a wee thing and sweet. I love him, and it was just like Angus to come up with the idea. Today my world is blessed and full of peace.

Praise be to the Goddess for keeping us safe another year.

Praise be to Mother Earth for sharing her bounty far and near.

*Praise be to magick, from which all blessings flow.*

*Praise be to my heart; I will follow where it goes.*

*Blessed be.*

*— Bradhadair*

*Now Dagda is mewing to go out!*


"What's wrong?" Robbie demanded in the car.

I sniffled and wiped my hand over my face. "Oh, Alyce was telling me a sad story about some witches who died."

His eyes narrowed. "And you're crying because . . . ," he prompted.

"It just got to me," I said, trying to sound light. "I'm so tenderhearted."

"Okay, don't tell me," he said, sounding irritated. He started the car and began the drive back to Widow's Vale.

"It's just . . . I can't talk about it yet, okay, Robbie?" I almost whispered.

He was quiet for a few moments, then nodded. "Okay. But if you ever need a shoulder, I'm here."

It was so sweet of him that a wave of warmth rushed over me. I reached out to pat his shoulder. "Thanks. That helps. Really."

Darkness fell as we drove, and by the time we got back to school, streetlights were on. My thoughts had been churning around my birth mother's fate, and I was surprised to recognize the school building when Robbie stopped and I saw my car sitting by itself on the street.

"Thanks for the ride," I said. It was dark, and leaves were blowing off trees, flitting through the air. One brushed against me, and I flinched.

"You okay?" he asked.

"I think so. Thanks again. I'll see you tomorrow," I said, and got in Das Boot.

I felt like I had lived through my birth mother's story. She had to be the same Maeve Riordan on my birth certificate. She had to be. I tried to remember if I had seen the place of birth—if it had been Meshomah Falls or Widow's Vale. I couldn't remember. Did my parents know any of this story? How had they found me? How had I been adopted? The same old questions.

I started my car, feeling anger come over me again. They had the answers, and they were going to tell me. Tonight. I couldn't go through another day without knowing.

At home I parked and stormed up the front walk, already forming the words I was going to say, the questions I would ask. I pushed through the front door—

And found Aunt Eileen and her girlfriend, Paula Steen, sitting on the couch.

"Morgan!" said Aunt Eileen, holding out her arms. "How's my favorite niece?"

I hugged her as Mary K. said, "She said the exact same thing to me."

Aunt Eileen laughed. "You're both my favorite nieces."

I smiled, trying to mentally switch gears. A confrontation with my parents was out for now. And then—it was only then that I realized that Aunt Eileen knew I was adopted. Of course she did. She's my mom's sister. In fact, all of my parents' friends must know. They had always lived here in Widow's Vale, and unless my mom had faked a pregnancy, which I couldn't see her doing, they would all know that I had just turned up out of nowhere. And then two years later she really had had a baby: Mary K. Oh my God, I thought, appalled. I was utterly, utterly humiliated and embarrassed.

"Listen, we brought Chinese food," said Aunt Eileen, standing up.

"It's ready!" Mom called from the dining room. I would have given anything not to have to go in, but there was no way to get out of it. We all swarmed in. White cartons and plastic foam containers filled the center of the table.

"Hi," Mom said to me, scanning my face. "You got back in time."

"Uh-huh," I said, not meeting her gaze. "I was with Robbie."

"Robbie looks amazing lately," said Mary K., helping herself to some orange beef. "Has he been seeing a new dermatologist?"

"Um, I don't know," I said vaguely. "His skin has gotten a lot better."

"Maybe he's just grown out of it," suggested my mom. I couldn't believe she was making polite chitchat. Frustration started to boil in me as I tried to choke down my dinner.

"Can you pass the pork?" my dad asked.

For a while we all ate. If Aunt Eileen and Paula noticed that things were a bit weird, if we were stilted and less talkative, they didn't show it. But even Mary K., as naturally perky as she is, was holding back.

"Oh, Morgan, Janice called," said my dad. I could tell he was striving for a normal tone. "She wants you to call her back. I said you would, after dinner."

"Okay, thanks," I said. I stuffed a big bite of scallion pancake in my mouth so it wouldn't seem weird that I was being so quiet.

After dinner Aunt Eileen stood up and went into the kitchen, returning with a bottle of sparkling cider and a tray of glasses.

"What's all this?" my mom asked with a surprised smile.

"Well," Aunt Eileen said shyly as Paula got up to stand next to her. "We have some very exciting news."

Mary K. and I exchanged glances.

"We're moving in together," Eileen announced, her face full of happiness. She smiled at Paula, and Paula gave her a hug.

"I've already put my apartment on the market, and we're looking for a house," said Paula.

"Oh, awesome," said Mary K., getting up to hug Aunt Eileen and Paula. They beamed. I stood up and hugged them, too, and so did Mom. Dad hugged Eileen and shook Paula's hand.

"Well, this is lovely news," said Mom, although something in her face said that she thought it would be better if they had known each other longer.

Eileen popped the cork on the sparkling cider and poured it. Paula handed glasses around, and Mary K. and I immediately gulped down sips.

"Are you going to buy a house together or rent?" Mom asked.

"We're looking to buy," said Eileen. "We both have apartments now, but I want to get a dog, so we need a yard."

"And I need room for a garden," said Paula.

"A dog and a garden might be mutually exclusive," said my dad, and they laughed. I smiled, too, but it all felt so unreal: as if I were watching someone else's family on television.

"I was hoping you could help us with the house hunting," Eileen said to my mom.

Mom smiled, for the first time since yesterday, I realized. "I was already running through possibilities in my head," she admitted. "Can you come by the office soon, and we can set up some appointments?"

"That would be great," said Eileen. Paula reached over and squeezed her shoulder. They looked at each other as if no one else was in the room.

"Moving is going to be insane," said Paula. "I have stuff scattered everywhere: my mom's, my dad's, my sister's. My apartment was just too small to hold everything."

"Fortunately, I have a niece who's not only strong but has a huge car," Aunt Eileen offered brightly, looking over at me.

I stared at her. I wasn't really her niece, though, was I? Even Eileen had been playing into this whole fantasy that was my life. Even she, my favorite aunt, had been lying and keeping secrets from me for sixteen years.

"Aunt Eileen, do you know why Mom and Dad never told me I was adopted?" I just put it out there, and it was as if I had mentioned I had the bubonic plague.

Everyone stared at me, except Mary K., who was staring at her plate miserably, and Paula, who was watching Aunt Eileen with a concerned expression.

Aunt Eileen looked like she had swallowed a frog. Her eyes wide, she said, "What?" and shot quick glances at my mom and dad.

"I mean, don't you think somebody should have told me? Maybe just mentioned it? You could have said something. Or maybe you just didn't think it was that important," I pressed on. Part of me knew I wasn't being fair. But somehow I couldn't stop myself. "No one else seems to. After all, it's just my life we're talking about."

Mom said, "Morgan," in a defeated tone of voice.

"Uh . . . ," said Aunt Eileen, for once at a loss for words.

Everyone was as embarrassed as I was, and the festive air had gone out of dinner.

"Never mind," I said abruptly, standing up. "We can talk about it later. Why not? After sixteen years what's a few days more?"

"Morgan, I always felt your parents should be the ones to tell you—," Aunt Eileen said, sounding distressed.

"Yeah, right," I said rudely. "When was that going to happen?"

Mary K. gasped, and I pushed my chair back roughly. I couldn't stand being here one more second. I couldn't take their hypocrisy anymore. I would explode.

This time I remembered to grab my jacket before I ran out to my car and peeled off into the darkness.

# 9

# Healing Light

St. Patrick's Day, 1981

Oh, Jesus, Mary, and Joseph, I'm so drunk, I can hardly write. Ballynigel just put on a St. Paddy's party to end all parties. All the townspeople, everyone, gathered together to have a good time in the village. Human or witch, we all agree on St. Paddy's Day, the wearing of the green.

Pat O'Hearn dyed all his beer green, and it was sloshing into mugs, into pails, into shoes, anything. Old Towson gave some to his donkey, and that donkey has never been so tame or good-natured! I laughed until I had to hold my sides in.

The Irish Cowboys played their music all afternoon right in the town green, and we all danced and pinched one another, and the kids were throwing cabbages and potatoes. We had a good day, and our dark time seems to be well and truly over.

Now I'm home, and I lit three green candles to the Goddess

for prosperity and happiness. There's a full moon tonight, so I have to sober up, dress warm, and go gather my luibh. The dock root down at the pond is ready for taking in, and there's early violets, dandelions, and cattails, too, ready. I can't drink any more beer until then, or they'll find me facedown in the marsh, too drunk to pick myself up! What a day!

    — Bradhadair

As I drove it occurred to me that there was nowhere to go at eight o'clock on a Monday night in Widow's Vale, New York. I pictured myself showing up at Schweikhardt's soda shop, on Main Street, with tears streaming down my cheeks. I pictured myself showing up at Janice's the same way. No— Janice had no idea how complicated my life had gotten. Robbie? I considered for a second but shook my head. I hated going to his house, with his dad drinking beer in front of the TV and his mom all tight-lipped and angry. And of course Bree didn't even enter into it—God, what a bitch she'd been today.

Cal? I turned and headed toward his neighborhood, feeling desperate and daring, brave and terrified. Was I being presumptuous by going to his house uninvited? There was so much going on in my mind: my birth parents' story, my other parents' refusal to tell me the truth about my past, Bree—it was all too much to think about. I felt like I couldn't make any kind of decision about anything—even about whether it was okay for me to show up at Cal's house unannounced.

By the time I pulled into the long, cobblestone driveway of Cal's big stone house, I felt completely incoherent. What was I doing? I just wanted to drive off into the night forever, far away from everyone I knew. Be a different person. I couldn't believe this was my life.

I cut the lights and the engine and hunched over my steering wheel, literally frozen with uncertainty. I couldn't even start the car again to get out of there.

Who knows how long I huddled in the darkness outside Cal's home. I finally looked up when strong headlights flooded the interior of my car, reflecting off my rearview mirror and shining into my eyes. An expensive-looking SUV pulled around my car and parked neatly, close to the house. Its door opened, and a tall, slender woman stepped out, her hair barely visible in the darkness. The house's outdoor floodlights came on, bathing the driveway in warm yellow light. The woman walked to my car.

Feeling like an idiot, I rolled down my window as Selene Belltower approached. For long moments she gazed at my face, as if evaluating me. We neither smiled nor spoke to each other.

Finally she said, "Why don't you come inside, Morgan? You must be chilled through. I'll make some cocoa." As if it was normal to find a girl in a car sitting in the dark outside her house.

I got out of Das Boot and slammed the door. We walked up the broad stone steps together, Cal's mom and I, and through the massive wooden front door. She led me across the foyer, down a hall, into a huge French country–style kitchen I hadn't seen on my other visit here.

"Sit down, Morgan," she said, gesturing to a tall stool by the kitchen island.

I sat, hoping Cal was here. I hadn't seen his car outside, but maybe it was in the garage.

I cast my senses out, but I couldn't feel his presence close by. Selene Belltower's head snapped up as she poured milk into a pan. Her brows came together, and she looked at me assessingly.

"You're very strong," she commented. "I didn't learn how to cast my senses until I was in my twenties. Cal isn't here, by the way."

"I'm sorry," I said awkwardly. "I should go. I don't want to bother you. . . ."

"You're not bothering me," she said. She spooned some cocoa powder into the milk and whisked it smooth on the cooktop across from me. "I've been curious. Cal has told me some very interesting things about you."

Cal talked to his mother about me?

She laughed, a warm, earthy laugh, when she saw the expression on my face. "Cal and I are pretty close," she said. "For a long time it's been just the two of us. His father left us when Cal was about four."

"I'm sorry," I said again. She was speaking to me as if I were an adult, and for some reason this made me feel younger than sixteen.

Selene Belltower shrugged. "I was sorry, too. Cal missed his father very much, but he lives in Europe now, and they don't see each other often. At any rate—you shouldn't be startled that my son confides in me. It would be silly for him to try to hide anything, after all."

I breathed in, trying to relax. So this was life in a blood-witch household. No secrets.

Cal's mother poured the cocoa into two brightly colored hand-painted mugs and handed one to me. It was too hot to drink, so I set it down and waited. Selene waved her hand over her mug twice, then took a sip.

"Try this," she suggested, looking up at me. "Take your left hand and circle it widdershins over your mug. Say, 'Cool the fire.'"

I did, wondering. I felt warmth go into my left hand.

"Try the cocoa now," she said, watching me.

I took a sip. It was noticeably cooler, perfect to drink. I grinned, delighted.

"Left hand takes away," she explained. "Right hand gives. Deasil for increasing, widdershins for decreasing. And simple words are best."

I nodded and drank my cocoa. This one small thing was so fascinating to me. The idea that I could speak words, make movements that cooled a hot drink to the right temperature!

Selene smiled, and then her eyes focused on mine sympathetically. "You look like you've had a rough time."

This was an understatement, but I nodded. "Has Cal . . . told you about . . . anything?"

She put her mug down. "He's told me you recently found out you were adopted," she said. "That your biological parents must be blood witches. And this afternoon he told me you thought you were probably the daughter of two Irish witches who died here sixteen years ago."

I nodded again. "Not exactly here—Meshomah Falls. About two hours away. I think my mother's name was Maeve Riordan."

Selene's face became grave. "I've heard that story," she said. "I remember when it happened. I was forty years old;

Cal wasn't quite two. I remember thinking that such a thing could never happen to me, my husband, our child." Her long fingers played with the rim of her mug. "I know better now." She looked up at me again. "I'm very sorry this has happened to you. It's always somewhat difficult to be different, even if you have a lot of support. One is still set apart. But I know you must be having an especially hard time."

My throat felt like it was closing again, and I drank my cocoa. I didn't trust myself to agree. I distracted myself with pointless details: If she had been forty sixteen years ago, she would be about fifty-six now. She looked like she was about thirty-five.

"If you want," said Selene, sounding hesitant, "I can help you feel better."

"What do you mean?" I asked. For a wild moment I wondered, Is she offering me drugs?

"Well, I'm picking up waves of upset, discord, unhappiness, anger," she said. "We could make a small, two-person circle and try to get you to a better place."

I caught my breath. I had only ever made a circle with Cal and our coven. What would it be like with someone who was even more powerful than he was? I found myself saying, "Yes, please, if you don't mind."

Selene smiled, looking very much like Cal. "Come on, then."

The house was shaped like a U, with a middle part and two wings. She led me to the back of the left wing, through a very large room that I figured she must use for her coven's circles. She opened a door that set into the wall paneling, so you could barely see it. I felt a thrill of pure, childlike delight. Secret doors!

We stepped into a much smaller, cozier room furnished only with a narrow table, some bookshelves, and candelabras on the walls. Selene lit the candles.

"This is my private sanctuary," she said, brushing her fingers over the doorjamb. For a fleeting moment I saw sigils glimmering there. They must be for privacy or protection. But I had no idea how to read them. There was so much I needed to learn. I was a complete novice.

Selene had already drawn a small circle on the wooden floor, using a reddish powder that gave off a strong, spicy scent. She motioned me into the circle with her and then closed it behind us.

"Let's sit down," she said. With us facing each other, sitting cross-legged on the floor, there was very little room inside the circle.

We each sprinkled salt around our half of the circle, saying, "With this salt, I purify my circle."

Then Selene closed her eyes and let her head droop, her hands on her knees as if doing yoga. "With every breath out, release a negative emotion. With every breath in, take in white light, healing light, soothing and calming light. Feel it enter your fingers, your toes, settle in your stomach, reach up through the crown of your head."

As she spoke her voice became slower, deeper, more mesmerizing. My eyes were closed, my chin practically resting on my chest. I breathed out, forcing air completely out of my lungs. Then I breathed in, listening to her soothing words.

"I release tension," she murmured, and I repeated it after her without hesitation.

"I release fear and anger," she said, her words floating to me on a sea of calm. I repeated it and literally felt the knots in my stomach begin to uncoil, the tightness in my arms and calves unravel.

"I release uncertainty," she said, and I followed her.

We breathed deeply, silently for several minutes. My headache dissolved, my temples ceased throbbing, my chest expanded, and I could breathe more easily.

"I feel calm," Selene said.

"Me too," I agreed dreamily. I sensed rather than saw her smile.

"No, say it," she prompted, humor in her voice.

"Oh. I feel calm," I said.

"Open your eyes. Make this symbol with your right hand," she prompted, drawing in the air with two fingers. "It's the rune for comfort."

I watched her, then carefully drew in the air one straight line down, then a small triangle attached to the top, like a little flag.

"I feel at peace," she said, drawing the same rune on my forehead.

"I feel at peace," I said, feeling her finger trace heat on my skin. The memory of what had happened to my birth parents receded into the distance. I was aware of it, but it had less power to hurt me.

"I am love. I am peace. I am strength."

I said the words, feeling a delicious warmth flow over me.

"I call on the strength of the Goddess and the God. I call on the power of the Earth Mother," said Selene, tracing another rune onto my forehead. This one felt like half of a lopsided rectangle, and as it sank into my skin I thought, Strength.

Selene and I were joined. I could feel her strength inside

my head, feel her smoothing every wrinkle in my emotions, searching out every knot of fear, every snarl of anger. She probed deeper and deeper, and languidly I let her. She soothed away the pain until I was almost in a trance.

Ages later, I seemed to come awake again. Unbidden, I opened my eyes in time to see her raising her head and opening hers. I felt a little groggy and so much better, I couldn't help smiling. She smiled back.

"All right now?" she said softly.

"Oh, yes," I said, unable to put my feelings into words.

"Here's one more for you," she said, and she traced two triangles, touching, onto the backs of my hands. "That's for new beginnings."

"Thank you," I said, awed by her power. "I feel much better."

"Good." We stood, and she dissolved the circle and blew out the candles mounted around the small room. As we passed through the larger coven's room I saw a reflection of Selene's face in a huge, gilt-frame wall mirror. She was smiling. Her face was bright, almost triumphant as she led the way back to the foyer. Then the image was gone, and I thought I must have imagined it.

At the front door she patted my arm, and I thanked her again. Then I practically floated to my car, not feeling the slightest bit of November wind, November chill. I felt absolutely perfect all the way home. I didn't even wonder where Cal had been.

# 10

# Split

August 14, 1981

The coven over at Much Bencham has three new students, they tell us. We have none. Tara and Cliff were the last to join Belwicket as students, and that was three years ago. Until Lizzie Sims turns fourteen in four years, we have no one. Of course, at Much Bencham they take almost anyone who wants to study.

I say we should do the same—if we could even convince anyone to join us. Belwicket chose its own path long ago, and it is not for everyone. But we must expand. If we stick to only blood-born, clan-born witches, we will surely die out. We must seek out others of our kind, mingle clans. But Ma and the elders have shot me down time and again. They want us to remain pure. They refuse to let outsiders in.

Maybe some in Belwicket would rather die.
— Bradhadair

When I got home that night, my parents' light was already out, and if my car's rumbling engine woke them up, they didn't show it. Mary K. had waited up for me, listening to music in her room. She looked up and took off her headphones when I poked my head in.

"Hi," I said, feeling a deep love for her. After all, she'd always been my sister, if not by blood, then by circumstance. I regretted hurting her.

"Where did you go?" she asked.

"To Cal's. He wasn't there, but I talked to his mom."

Mary K. paused. "It was awful after you left. I thought Mom was going to burst into tears. Everyone was really embarrassed."

"I'm sorry," I said sincerely. "It's just that I can't believe Mom and Dad kept this to themselves my whole life. They lied to me." I shook my head. "Tonight I realized that Aunt Eileen, and our other relatives, and Mom and Dad's friends *all* know I'm adopted. I just felt so stupid for not knowing myself. I was just . . . furious that they never told me when all these other people know."

"Yeah, I hadn't thought of that," said Mary K., frowning slightly. "But you're right. They would all know." She looked at me. "*I* didn't know. You believe that, don't you?"

I nodded. "There's no way *you'd* be able to keep a secret like that." I smiled as Mary K. aimed her pillow at me.

The blanket of peace, forgiveness, and love that Selene Belltower had wrapped around over me was still cocooning me in its comfortable embrace. "Look, it's going to be pretty awful for a while. Mom and Dad have to tell me about my past and how I was adopted. I can't stop till I know. But it doesn't mean I don't love you or them. We'll get through it somehow," I said.

Uncertainty played across Mary K.'s pretty face. "Okay," she said, accepting my word.

"I'm happy about Aunt Eileen and Paula," I said, changing the subject.

"Me too. I didn't want Aunt Eileen to be alone anymore," said Mary K. "Do you think they'll have kids?"

I laughed. "First things first. They need to live together for a while."

"Yeah. Oh, well. I'm tired." Mary K. took off her headphones and dropped them on the floor.

"Here, let me do this." Reaching over, I gently traced the rune for comfort on her forehead, the way Selene had showed me. I felt the warmth leave my fingertips and stood back to see Mary K. looking at me unhappily.

"Please don't do that to me," she whispered. "I don't want to be part of it."

Stung, I blinked, then nodded. "Yeah, sure," I mumbled. I turned and fled to my own room, feeling dismayed. Something that had given me joy was only upsetting to my sister. It was a clear sign of the differences between us, the growing space that pushed her in one direction and me in another.

That night I slept deeply, without dreams, and woke up feeling wonderful. I put my hands together as if I could still see the sigil traced there: Daeg. A new dawn. An awakening.

"Morgan?" Mary K. called from the hallway. "Come on. School."

I was already shoving my feet into my slippers. No doubt I was running late, as usual. I rushed through my shower, threw on some clothes, and pounded downstairs, my wet hair practically strangling me. In the kitchen I grabbed a breakfast bar, ready to dash out the door. Mary K. looked up calmly from her orange juice.

"No hurry," she said. "I got you up early for once. I've been late twice in the last month."

Mouth open, I looked at the clock. School didn't start for almost forty-five minutes! I sank into a chair and waved incoherently at the fridge.

Taking pity on me, my sister reached in and handed me a Diet Coke. I gulped it down, then stomped back upstairs to untangle my hair.

Somehow, we were late anyway. At school I parallel parked my car with practiced efficiency. Then I spotted Bakker, coming toward the car to meet Mary K. My mood soured.

"Look, there he is," I said. "Lying in wait like a spider."

Mary K. punched my leg. "Stop it," she said. "I thought you liked him."

"He's okay," I said. I've got to chill, I thought. I'd be so peeved if anyone tried to pull the big-sister routine on me. But I couldn't help asking, "Does he know you're only fourteen?"

Mary K. rolled her eyes. "No, he thinks I'm a junior," she said sarcastically. "Don't let the cat out of the bag." She got out of the car. As she and Bakker kissed, I slammed my car door shut and hitched my backpack onto my shoulder. Then I headed toward the east door.

"Oh, Morgan, wait!" someone called. I turned and spotted Janice Yutoh, her hair bouncing as she hurried toward me. Whoops—I'd totally forgotten to return her call the night before.

"Sorry I spaced on calling you," I said as she caught up to me.

She waved a hand in the air. "No biggie. I just wanted to say hi," she said, panting slightly. "I haven't seen you at all lately, except in class."

"I know," I said apologetically. "A lot of stuff's been going on." This was such a lame representation of the truth that I almost laughed. "My aunt Eileen is moving in with her girl-friend," I said, thinking of one bright spot.

"That's great! Tell her I'm happy for her," said Janice.

"Will do," I said. "What'd you get on Fishman's essay test?"

"I somehow pulled an A out of my hat," she said as we walked toward the main building.

"Cool. I got a B-plus. I hate essay tests. Too many words," I complained. Janice laughed. Then we saw Tamara and Ben Reggio heading into the main door just as the bell rang.

"Gotta catch Ben," said Janice, moving off. "He's got my Latin notes."

"See you in class." I went in through the east door, where the coven had started to meet in the mornings, but the cement benches were empty. Cal must have gone inside already. My disappointment at not seeing him was almost equaled by my relief at not having to face Bree.

By lunchtime it was drizzling outside, with sullen rivulets tracing lines on the windows. I filed into the lunchroom, for once grateful for its warm, steamy atmosphere. By the time I collected a tray and looked around, most of the coven was sitting at a table closest to the windows. Raven and Bree weren't there, I saw with a lift of relief. Neither was Beth Nielson.

I made my way over and sat down next to Cal. When he smiled, it was like the sun coming out.

"Hi," he said, making space for me on the table. "Did you get here late this morning?"

I nodded, opening my soda. "Just as the bell rang."

"Can I have a fry?" he asked, taking one without waiting for my answer. I felt a warm glow at his easy familiarity.

"Mom told me you dropped by last night," he said. "I'm sorry I missed you." He squeezed my knee under the table. "You okay?" he asked softly.

"Yeah, your mom was really nice. She showed me some rune magick," I said, dropping my voice.

"Cool," Jenna said, leaning over the table. "Like what?"

"A few different runes for different things," I said. "Like runes for happiness, starting over, peace and calm."

"Did they work?" asked Ethan.

"Yes!" I said, laughing. As if a spell by Selene Belltower wouldn't work. "It would be great if we could start learning about runes, everything about them."

Cal nodded. "Runes are really powerful," he said. "They've been used for thousands of years. I have some books on them if you want to borrow them."

"I'd like to read them, too," said Sharon, stirring her straw around in her milk carton.

"Here's a rune for you guys," said Cal. He cleared a space in the center of the table and traced an image with his finger. It looked like two parallel lines with two other lines crossed between them, joining them. He drew it several times until we could all picture it.

"What does that mean?" asked Matt.

"Basically it means interdependence," Cal explained. "Community. Feeling goodwill toward your kinsmen and kinswomen. It's how we all feel about each other, our circle. Cirrus."

We all looked at each other for a minute, letting this sink in.

"God, there's so much to learn," said Sharon. "I feel like I'll never be able to put it all together—herbs, spells, runes, potions."

"Can I talk to you?" Beth Nielson had walked up and now stood in front of Cal, a multicolored crocheted cap covering her short hair.

"Sure," said Cal. He looked more closely at her. She was frowning. "Do you want to go somewhere private?"

"No." Beth shook her head, not looking at him. "It doesn't matter. They can hear it."

"What's wrong, Beth?" Cal asked quietly. Somehow we all heard him, even over the din of the lunchroom.

Beth shrugged and looked away. Glittery aqua eye shadow glowed above her eyes and contrasted sharply with her coffee-colored skin. She sniffed, as if she had a cold.

Across the table I looked at Jenna. She raised her eyebrows at me.

"It's just—the whole thing doesn't feel right to me," Beth said. "I thought it would be cool, you know? But it's all too weird. Doing circles. Morgan making flowers bloom," she said, gesturing to me. "It's too strange." She raised her shoulders beneath her brown leather jacket and let them fall. "I don't want anything more to do with it. I don't like it. It feels wrong." Her nose ring twinkled under the fluorescent lights.

"That's too bad," said Cal. "Wicca isn't intended to make anyone uncomfortable. It's meant to make you celebrate the beauty and power of the earth."

Beth gave him a blank look, as if to say, Come on.

"So you want to quit the coven. Are you sure about this?" Cal asked. "Maybe you just need more time to get used to it."

Beth shook her head. "No. I don't want to do it anymore."

"Well, if Wicca isn't for you, then that's your choice. Thanks for being honest," Cal said.

"Uh-huh," said Beth, shifting her weight from one Doc Marten to the other.

"Beth, one thing," Cal said. "Please respect our privacy." There was a serious note in his voice that made Beth look up.

"You've come to our circles; you've felt magick's power," Cal went on. "Keep those experiences to yourself, okay? They're no one's business but ours."

"Yeah, okay," Beth said, looking at Cal.

"Well," Cal said. "It's your decision to go. But just remember that the circle won't be open to you again if you change your mind. Sorry, but that's how it works."

"I'm not changing my mind," said Beth. She moved off without looking back.

For a few moments we all looked around at each other.

"What was that about?" I asked.

Jenna coughed. "Yeah, that was pretty weird."

"Don't know," said Cal. A shadow crossed his face. Then he

seemed to shrug it off. "But like I said, Wicca isn't for every-one." He leaned forward. "I thought at our next circle, I could show you guys some more runes and maybe a small spell."

"All right," Ethan said. "Cool." He leaned across to Sharon. "Are you gonna eat that brownie?"

She made a pained face, but I could tell she was kidding. "Yes."

"Halfies?" he asked. Ethan, former pothead, now merely scruffy underdog, grinned coyly at Sharon. It was like watching a street mongrel trying to flirt with a well-groomed poodle.

"I'll give you a tiny bite," Sharon said, breaking off a piece. Her cheeks were slightly pink.

Ethan grinned more broadly and popped the brownie morsel into his mouth.

Around us hundreds of students filed to and from tables, eating, talking to one another, busing their trays. We were a small, private microcosm of the school. To me it felt like we were the only ones talking about things that really mat-tered—things that were far more important and interesting than the latest pep squad rally or prom theme contest. I couldn't wait to be finished with high school, to move on with the rest of my life. I saw myself devoted to Wicca, still with Cal, living a life full of meaning and joy and magick.

Robbie's elbow knocking into me jolted me out of my daydream.

"Sorry," he said, rubbing his temples. "Do you have any Tylenol?"

"Nope, sorry. Your doctor's appointment is today, right?" I asked him, then took a bite of hamburger.

"Yeah."

"Here, take this." Jenna rummaged in her purse and took out two tablets.

Robbie squinted at them, then tossed them down with the rest of his soda. "What was that?"

"Cyanide," said Sharon, and we laughed.

"Actually, it was Midol," Jenna said, turning away to give another cough. I wondered if she was getting sick.

Matt whooped with laughter as Robbie gaped at her in dismay.

"It'll really help," Jenna insisted. "It's what I take for my headaches."

"Oh, man." Robbie shook his head. I was almost doubled over with laughter.

"Look at it this way," said Cal brightly. "You won't get that awful bloated feeling."

"You'll feel pretty all day," suggested Matt, laughing so hard, he had to wipe his eyes.

"Oh, man," said Robbie again as we cackled.

"Well, this is nice," came Raven's snide voice. "Everyone all happy and laughing together. Cozy, huh, Bree?"

"Very cozy," said Bree.

I stopped laughing and looked up at them, standing by our lunch table. People streamed by in back of them, making Bree edge closer to me. I still felt profoundly relaxed, thanks to Selene, and as I gazed at my former best friend, I couldn't help missing her powerfully. She was so familiar to me—I had known her before she was beautiful, when she was just a pretty little girl. She'd never gone through an awful awkward stage, like most kids, but when she was twelve, she'd had braces and a bad haircut. I had known her before she liked boys, while her mother and brother still lived at home.

So much had changed.

"Hi, Raven, Bree," Cal said, still smiling. "Grab some chairs—we'll make room."

Raven took out one of her foul-smelling Gauloises and tapped it against her wrist. "No, thanks. Did Beth tell you she was ditching the coven?" she asked, her voice seeming harsh and unfriendly. I glanced at Bree, who was keeping her eyes on Raven.

"Yes, she did," Cal replied, shrugging. "Why?"

Raven and Bree looked at each other. A month ago, Bree and I were making fun of Raven together. Now they acted like best friends. I tried hard to hold on to my feelings of calm and peace.

Bree gave Raven a tiny nod, and Raven's lips thinned in what could pass for a smile.

"We're leaving, too," she announced.

I know my surprise showed on my face, and when I quickly surveyed the table, there was no mistaking that it was shared. Next to me Cal was suddenly alert, frowning as he looked at them.

"No," said Robbie. "Come on."

"Why?" Jenna asked. "I thought you were both so into it."

"We are into it," Raven said pointedly. "We're just not into you." She tapped her cigarette harder, and I could practically feel how much she wanted to light it up.

"We've joined a different coven," Bree announced. The expression on her face made me think of a kid I had baby-sat once. He had once thrown a live lizard onto the dining room table, during a meal, just to see what would happen.

"A different coven!" exclaimed Sharon. She twitched her short suede skirt down, bracelets jangling. "What different coven?"

"A different one," said Raven in a bored tone. She raised one shoulder and let it drop.

"Bree, don't be stupid," said Robbie, and his words seemed to hurt her.

"We've started our own group," Bree told Robbie, and Raven glanced at her sharply. I wondered if Bree had been supposed to keep that secret.

"Started your own?" Cal said, rubbing his chin. "What is wrong with Cirrus?"

"To tell you the truth, Cal," Bree said coldly, "I don't want to be in a coven with backstabbers and betrayers. I need to be able to trust the people I do magick with."

This was aimed at me, and possibly at Cal, and I felt heat rise in my cheeks.

Cal raised his eyebrows. "Yes, trust is really important," he said slowly. "I agree with you there. Are you sure you can trust the people in your new coven?"

"Yes," said Raven, a bit too loudly. "It's not like you're the only witch in town, you know."

"No, no, I'm not," Cal agreed. I heard a hint of annoyance in his voice. He put his arm around my shoulders. "For example, there's Morgan here. Does your new coven have any blood witches?"

All eyes turned to me.

"Blood witch?" asked Bree, derision in her voice.

"You said that on Samhain," remembered Raven. "You were just yanking our chains."

"I wasn't," Cal said. I swallowed and looked down, hoping

this conversation would stop before people followed it to its logical conclusion.

"If she's a blood witch," Bree all but snarled, "then so are her parents, right? Isn't that what you told us? I mean, am I supposed to believe that Sean and Mary Grace Rowlands are blood witches?"

Cal went silent, as if he just at that moment realized what this could lead to. "Whatever," he said, and I leaned against him, knowing he was trying to protect me.

"Anyway," said Cal. "Let's not get off the subject. So you really want out of the coven?"

"Out and about, baby," said Raven, putting her unlit cigarette in her mouth.

"Bree, think about what you're doing," Robbie urged her, and I was glad he was trying to talk her out of it since I couldn't.

"I have thought," said Bree. "I want out."

"Well, be careful," said Cal, standing up. I stood up, too, grabbing my purse and my lunch tray. "Remember, most witches are good, but not all of them. Make sure you haven't left the frying pan for the fire."

Raven gave a short bark of a laugh. "How pithy. Thanks for the advice."

Cal gave them a last, considering look, then nodded at me. We walked away from the group. I dumped my tray at the bus bin, and we left the lunchroom, heading for the main building.

Cal walked with me to my locker. I spun the combination and opened the door while he waited.

"If they make a new coven, will it affect us somehow?" I asked, my voice low.

Cal brushed back his dark hair and shrugged. "I don't think so," he said. "It's just . . ." He pinched his lip with two fingers, thinking.

"What?"

"Well, I wonder who they're working with," he said. "They're obviously not doing this by themselves. I hope they're being careful. Not every witch is . . . benign."

I felt tension weave its way into my short-held peace and looked at Cal. He kissed me, warmth in his golden eyes.

"See you later." A flashing grin, and he was gone.

# 11

# Connected

January 3, 1982

Old Towson lost three more sheep last night. This is after all the ward-evil spells we've been doing for the past month. Now most of his flock is gone, and he's not the only one. He said today in the Eagle and Hare that he's wiped out — doesn't have enough ewes left to start over. There's nothing for him to do except sell out.

I feel like all I do is go around doing warding spells. We're all paranoid and living under a dark shadow. For the past week I've been spelling Ma's leg after she broke it, bicycling to the village. But even with my spells she says it's hurting, not healing properly.

I want to get out of here. Being a witch is doing no one good nowadays and is doing a bushel of harm. It's like a film is over us, lessening our powers. I don't know what to do. Angus doesn't, either. He's worried, too, but he tries not to show it.

*Damnation! I thought the evil was behind us! Now it looks like it was only sleeping, sleeping among us, in our beds. Winter has awoken it. — Bradhadair*

On Wednesday morning, when I was toasting two Pop-Tarts for breakfast, I heard footsteps overhead.

"Mary K.!" I said. "Who's upstairs?"

Mary K. blinked. "Mom," she said, turning back to the comics. "She's staying home sick today."

I looked at the top of my sister's head. Mom never stayed home from work. She had been known to show houses in a snowstorm when she had the flu.

"What's wrong with her?" I asked. "She was fine last night, wasn't she?" She and my dad had had dinner out alone, something they almost never did. I had figured they were avoiding me, and I had waited up for them, but at eleven-thirty I had given up and gone to bed.

"I don't know. Maybe she just wanted a day off."

"Huh." Maybe this was my chance: I could go upstairs right now and get her to answer all my questions.

On the other hand, I would be late for school. And Cal was at school. Besides, if she wanted to tell me anything, she'd have told me by now. Right?

I sighed. Or maybe the truth was, now that the chance was staring me in the face, as it were, I was afraid to seize it. Scared of what I might learn.

My Pop-Tarts leaped energetically out of the toaster and broke on the kitchen counter. I gathered up the pieces in a paper towel and gave my sister a gentle kick.

"Let's go," I said. "Education awaits us." Mom would be

home when I got out of school. I could talk to her then.

Mary K. nodded and got into her coat.

As it turned out, my big confrontation didn't work out the way I'd planned. When I got home from school, I'd worked myself up for a real scene. I went up to Mom's room, threw open the door . . . and found her sound asleep. Her red hair lay across her pillow, and once again I noticed the silver strands in it. Was it my imagination, or were there more of them than even a couple of days before?

She looked so tired. I didn't have the heart to wake her.

I crept out like a mouse. Then Tamara called and asked if I could come over and study with her for a calc test. So I went. Anything to get out of the house.

I had dinner at Tamara's, and when I got home, Mom and Dad had both gone to bed.

I went into the study and switched on the computer. I wanted to go to one of the online Wicca sites and see if I could find out the meaning of the runes on Selene Belltower's door frame. I could still picture at least five of them in my mind. I also wanted to look up Maeve Riordan's family tree again. Maybe there was some link I hadn't noticed or some other information I'd missed.

While the computer booted up, I sat there, biting my thumbnail and thinking. Part of me was getting more and more wound up, the longer my parents avoided answering my questions. But I also had to admit that part of me was almost happy about these delays. I was honestly afraid of how painful and ugly the whole scene might be.

I logged on and entered in the html address that I remembered from before. But instead of Maeve's family tree a message popped onto the screen:

*The page cannot be displayed. The page you are looking for is currently unavailable. The Web site might be experiencing technical difficulties, or you may need to adjust your browser settings.*

I frowned. Had I entered the address wrong? I typed in *Maeve Riordan* and ran a search. Twenty-six matches popped up.

Last time there had been twenty-seven.

I scrolled rapidly down the list. No html. Was the genealogy site gone?

I tried running a search for *Ballynigel.* That took me to a map site and opened a window with a map of Ireland. Ballynigel was a dot on the west coast. I couldn't zoom in on it.

I typed in *Belwicket* and clicked the search button. I got no hits.

I slapped the keyboard in frustration. The site was gone. Just gone. As if it had never been there.

I told myself not to get too worked up. Maybe it was being upgraded or updated or something. If I just tried it again in a couple of days, it might well be back.

Closing my eyes for a moment, I tipped back my head and breathed deeply. Then, feeling calmer, I entered a Web address I'd gotten from Ethan—an address for a site about rune magick.

In a moment the home page opened, and mysterious symbols glowed before my eyes. I leaned closer, my worries fading to the back of my mind as I began to read.

It was nearly an hour later when I finally logged off and shut down the computer. When I closed my eyes, runes still danced across the insides of my lids. I'd learned a lot tonight.

I picked up a pen and traced my new favorite rune on a scrap of paper that sat by the keyboard. Ken: It looked like a V turned on its side. It stood for fire, including inspiration and passion of spirit. It was so simple, yet so strong.

Underneath it I traced my other new favorite rune, Ur, strength.

I sighed. I needed a lot of that right now.

On Thursday afternoon I was startled when Mom came into the family room. I was watching Oprah and doing my American history homework.

"Hi, Morgan," she said, sounding tentative. Her hair was brushed and held back from her face by two combs. She wore no makeup, but she had on a sweat suit embroidered with leaves. "Where's Mary K.?"

"I dropped her at Jaycee's," I said.

"Oh, all right." Mom wandered over to the far wall and picked up a clay pot that I'd made in third grade, then set it back down on its shelf. "Hey, how come I haven't seen Bree around this week?"

I swallowed hard, replaying the scene yesterday in the cafeteria, when Bree and Raven had announced they were starting their own coven. I didn't think Bree would be spending a whole lot of time with me anymore.

But I didn't have the strength to get into it with Mom right now. So I just said, "I guess she's been pretty busy."

"Mmmm." To my surprise, Mom let it go at that. She prowled around the room some more, picking things up and putting them down. Then she said abruptly, "Mary K. says you have a boyfriend."

"Huh? Oh, yeah," I said in surprise, realizing she wasn't up

on the whole Cal thing. Of course. How could she have
been? Cal and my discovery about my birth happened at almost the same time.

"His name is Cal Blaire," I explained, feeling awkward.
First of all, we'd never talked about boys before. There had
never been anything to discuss. Second, why was I obligated
to tell her anything? She obviously had no problem keeping
secrets from me.

But still, I'd had sixteen years of thinking of her as my
mom. That habit was hard to break. "He and his mom moved
here in September," I added.

Mom leaned against the doorjamb. "What does he think
of witchcraft?"

I blinked and flicked off the TV. "Um, he likes it," I said
stiffly.

Mom nodded.

"Why didn't you ever tell me that I was adopted?" I said,
the words rushing out now that I had my chance.

I saw her swallow as she searched for an answer. "There
were some very good reasons at the time," she said finally.
The silence of the house seemed to underscore her words.

"Everyone says you're supposed to be open about it,"
I said. Already I could feel my throat getting tight, and suddenly my nerves felt like thorns.

"I know," Mom said quietly. "I know you want—need—
some answers."

"I deserve some answers!" I said, raising my voice. "You
and Dad lied to me for sixteen years! You lied to Mary K.!
And everyone else knew the truth!"

She shook her head, an odd look on her face. "No one

knows the whole truth," she said. "Not even your father and me."

"What does that mean?" I crossed my arms over my chest. I tried to hold on to my anger so I wouldn't cry.

"Your dad and I have been talking," she said. "We know you want to know. And we're going to tell you. Soon."

"When?" I snapped.

Mom gave an odd smile, as if at a private joke. She was being so calm and yet looked so fragile that it was hard for me to stay angry. There was nothing here to fight against, and that pissed me off even more.

"It's been sixteen years," she said gently. "Give us a few more days. I need time to think."

I stared at her in disbelief, but with that same odd smile she brushed her hand lightly against my cheek, then left the room.

For some reason, the memory of my sneaking into my parents' bed at night, when I was little, came into my mind. I used to worm my way in between them and go right to sleep. Nothing had ever felt so secure or so safe. Now it seemed strange. My childhood memories were being revised every day.

The phone rang, and I seized it like a lifeline. I knew it was Cal.

"Hi," said Cal, before I could speak, and a warm sense of comfort passed over me. "I miss you. Can I come over?"

I went from utter despair to pure joy in one second. "Actually, could I come over there?" I asked.

"You don't mind?"

"Oh, God, no. I'll be right there, okay?"

"Great," he said.

I flew from the house, rushing toward happiness.

Cal met me at the front door of his house. It was already almost dark, and the air felt heavy and damp, as if it might snow early this year.

"I can only stay a little while," I said, my breath puffing slightly.

"Thanks for coming," he said, leading me inside. "I could have come to your house."

I shook my head, taking off my coat. "You have more privacy here," I said. "Is your mom home?"

"No," said Cal as we started up the stairs to his room. "She's at the hospital with someone from her coven. I have to go over later and help her." It occurred to me that the two of us were alone in his house. A little shiver of anticipation went through me.

"I forgot to ask Robbie today," Cal said, opening the attic door to his room. "Is he getting new glasses?"

"I don't know. They're going to do more tests." I rubbed my arms as we walked into Cal's room, even though it was toasty warm. I felt comfortable here, with Cal. The rest of my life might be in turmoil, but here I knew I had power. And I knew Cal understood. It gave me a wonderful feeling of relief.

Looking around Cal's room, I remembered the night we had done a circle here and I had seen everyone's auras. It had been so seductive, being touched by magick. How could anyone not want to pursue it?

Behind me Cal touched my arm, and I turned to him. He

smiled at me. "I like having you here," he said. "And I'm glad you came. I wanted to give you something."

I looked up at him questioningly.

"Here." Reaching up, he untied the knot in the leather string around his neck. Its silver pentacle dangled, catching the lamplight and shining. This necklace had been one of the first things I'd noticed about him, and I remembered thinking how much I'd liked it. I stepped closer, and Cal fastened it around my neck. It fell to a point above my breastbone, and he traced around it on my shirt.

"Thank you," I whispered. "It's beautiful." Reaching up my hand, I curled it around his neck and pulled him to me. He met my kiss halfway.

"How are things at home?" Cal asked a moment later, still holding me.

I felt like I could tell him anything. "Strange," I said. I pulled myself out of his arms and walked around his room. "I've hardly seen my parents. Today Mom was home, and I asked her about being adopted, and she said she needed more time." I shook my head, looking at Cal's tall bookcase, its rows of books on witchcraft, spell making, herbs, runes. . . . I wanted to sit down and start reading and not get up for a long time.

"Every time I think about how they lied to me, I feel furious," I told Cal, my hands clenching into fists. I let out a breath. "But today my mom looked—I don't know. Older. Fragile, somehow."

I stopped next to Cal's bed. He walked over to me and rubbed my back. I took his hand and brought it to my cheek.

"Part of me feels like they're not my real family," I said.

"And another part of me thinks, of course they're my real family. They feel like my real family."

He nodded, his hand stroking up and down my arm. "It's strange when people you think you know really well feel suddenly different somehow."

He sounded like he was speaking from experience, and I looked up at him.

"Like my father," he said. "He was the high priest of my mom's coven when they were married. And he met another woman, another witch, in the coven. Mom and I used to make mean jokes about how she had put a love spell on him, but really, in the end, I think maybe he just . . . loved her more."

I heard the hurt in his voice and rested my head against his chest, my arms going around his waist.

"They live in northern England now," Cal went on. His chest vibrated against my ear as he spoke. "She had a son, my age, from her first marriage, and they've had, I think, two more kids together."

"That's awful," I said.

He breathed in and out slowly. "I don't know. Maybe I'm just used to it now. But I just think that's how it goes. Nothing is static; things always change. The best you can do is change along with them and work with what you have."

I was silent, thinking about my own situation.

"I think the important thing is to get through the anger and negative feelings because they get in the way of magick," Cal said. "It's hard, but sometimes you just have to decide to let those feelings go."

His voice trailed off, and we stood there comfortably for a while. Finally, reluctantly, I glanced at my watch.

"Speaking of going, I have to go," I said.

"Already?" Cal said, leaning down to kiss me. He murmured something against my lips.

Smiling, I wriggled out of his grasp. "What did you say?"

"Nothing." He shook his head. "I shouldn't have said anything."

"What?" I asked again, concerned now. "What's wrong?"

"Nothing's wrong," he said. "It's just . . . suddenly I thought of *mùirn beatha dàn.* You know."

I looked at him. "What? What are you talking about?"

"You know," he said again, sounding almost shy. "*Mùirn beatha dàn.* You've read about it, right?"

I shook my head. "What is it?"

"Um, soul mate," said Cal. "Life partner. Predestined mate."

My heart almost stopped beating, and my breath froze in my throat. I couldn't speak.

"In the form of Wicca that I practice," Cal explained, "we believe that for every witch, there's one true soul mate who's also a full-blooded witch; male or female, it doesn't matter. They're connected to that person, and belong together, and basically will only be truly happy with that person." He shrugged. "It sort of . . . came into my head just now, when we were kissing."

"I never heard of it," I whispered. "How do you know if it happens?"

Cal laughed wryly. "That's the tricky part. Sometimes it isn't that easy. And of course, people have strong wills: They can choose to be with people, insist on believing that this person is their *mùirn beatha dàn* when they're wrong and just won't admit it."

I wondered if he was talking about his mother and father.

"Is there any surefire way to tell?" I asked.

"I've heard of spells you can do: complicated ones. But mostly witches just rely on their feelings, their dreams, and their instincts. They just feel this person is the one, and they go with it."

I felt exhilarated, like I was about to take off and fly. "And do you think . . . maybe we're connected that way?" I asked breathlessly.

He touched my cheek. "I think we might be, yes," he said, his voice husky.

My eyes felt huge. "So what now?" I blurted out, and he laughed.

"We wait; we stay together. Finish growing up together."

This was such an amazing, wonderful, seductive idea that I wanted to shout, I love you! And we will always be together! I'm the one for you, and you're the one for me!

"How do you say it again?" I asked.

"*Mùirn beatha dàn,*" he said slowly, the words sounding ancient and lovely and mysterious.

I repeated them softly. "Yes," I said, and we met again in a kiss.

Long minutes later I pulled away from him. "Oh, no, I've really got to go! I'm going to be late!"

"Okay," he said, and we headed out of his room. It felt so hard to leave this place where everything felt so right. Especially when I knew I had to go home.

Again I thought about the first time I'd been in Cal's room, when the coven had met there. "Are you upset that Beth and Raven and Bree have quit?" I asked as we headed down the stairs.

He thought for a moment. "Yes and no," he said. "No because I don't think you should try to keep someone in a coven against their will or even if they're not very sure. It just makes negative energy. And yes because they were all kind of challenging personalities, and they added something to the mix. Which was good for the coven." He shrugged. "I guess we'll just have to wait and see what happens."

I put on my coat, wishing I didn't have to go out into the cold. Outside the trees were almost bare, and the leftover leaves were a faded brown everywhere I looked.

"Ugh," I said, glancing out at Das Boot.

"Fall is trying to turn into winter," said Cal, breathing steam in the chilly air.

I watched his chest rise and fall, and a bolt of desire ripped through me. I wanted so badly to touch him, to run my hands through his hair, down his back, to kiss his throat and chest. I wanted to be close to him. To be his *mùirn beatha dàn*.

Instead I tore myself away, fumbling in my coat pocket for my keys, leaving Cal standing in the light from his door. My heart was full and aching, and I felt heavy with magick.

# 12

# Beauty Out

*Imbolc, 1982*

*Oh, Goddess, Goddess, please help me. Please help me. Mathair, her hand rising up black from the smoking ashes. My little Dagda. My own da.*

*Oh, Goddess, I'm going to be ill; my soul is breaking. I cannot bear this pain.*

*— Bradhadair*

That night my parents tried to act normal at dinner, but I kept looking at them with questions in my eyes, and by dessert we were all staring at our plates. Mary K. was obviously upset by the silence, and as soon as dinner was over she went up to her room and started playing loud music. Ceiling-shaking thumps told us she was dancing out some of her stress.

I couldn't stand being there. If only Cal wasn't helping his mom. Impulsively I called Janice and joined her, Ben Reggio, and Tamara at the dollar movies up in Red Kill. We saw some stupid action movie that involved a lot of motorcycle chases. The whole time I sat there in the dark theater, I kept thinking, *mùirn beatha dàn*, over and over.

On Saturday morning Dad went outside to rake leaves and cut back the shrubs and trees so they wouldn't be broken in a winter ice storm. Mom took off after breakfast to go to her church women's club.

I put on my jacket and crunched my way outside to my dad.

"When are you guys going to tell me?" I said flatly. "Are you just going to pretend nothing happened?"

He paused and leaned on the rake for a moment. "No, Morgan," he said at last. "We couldn't do that, no matter how much we wanted to." His voice was mild, and again I felt some of my anger deflate. I was determined not to let it go and kicked at a small pile of leaves.

"Well?" I demanded. "Where did you get me? Who were my parents? Did you know them? What happened to them?"

Dad flinched as if my words were physically hurting him.

"I know we have to talk about it," he said, his voice thin and raspy. "But ... I need more time."

"Why?" I exploded, throwing my arms wide. "What are you waiting for?"

"I'm sorry, sweetheart," he said, looking down at the ground. "I know we've made a lot of mistakes in the past sixteen years. We tried to do our best. But Morgan." He looked at me. "We've buried this for sixteen years. It isn't easy to dredge it up. I know you want answers, and I hope we can give them to you. But it isn't easy.

And in the end, it might be that you wish you didn't know."

I gaped at him, then shook my head in disbelief and stalked back to the house. What was I going to do?

On Saturday night I dropped Mary K. off at her friend Jaycee's house. They were going to meet Bakker and a bunch of other people at the movies. I was going on to meet with our coven at Matt's house.

"Where's Bakker's car?" I asked as I pulled up in front of Jaycee's house.

Mary K. made a face. "His folks took it away for a week after he flunked a history exam."

"Oh, too bad," I said. "Well, have a good time. Don't do anything I wouldn't do."

Mary K. rolled her eyes. "Oh, okay," she said dryly. "Note to self: Try not to dance around naked, doing witchcraft. Thanks for the ride." She got out and slammed the car door, and I watched her go into Jaycee's house.

Sighing, I drove on to Matt's house, following his directions to the very outskirts of town. Ten minutes later I parked in front of a low-slung brick modern house, and Jenna let me in.

"Hey!" she said brightly. "Come on in. We're in the living room. I can't remember—have you ever been here before?"

"No," I said, leaving my coat on a metal hook. "Are Matt's parents here?"

Jenna shook her head. "His dad had a medical convention in Florida, and his mom went, too. We have the whole place to ourselves."

"Sweet," I said, following her. We took a right into a large living room, a white rectangle with one whole wall made of glass. I guess it must have looked out onto the backyard, but right now it was dark outside, and all I could see was our own reflections.

"Hi, Morgan," said Matt. He was wearing an old rugby shirt and jeans. "Welcome to Adler Hall."

We both laughed as Sharon came into the room. "Hi, Morgan," she said. "Matt, what's with all the bizarre furniture?"

"My mom is into sixties stuff," Matt explained.

Ethan poked his head up from a red plush couch. It was so deep, it looked like it was about to swallow him. A white floor lamp shaped like a globe with one flat side curved over his head. "I feel like I've gone back in time," he said. "All we need is a conversation pit."

"There's one in the study," said Matt, grinning.

The doorbell rang, and I felt a warm thrill of recognition even before Jenna went to answer it. Cal, I thought happily, a tingle going down my spine. *Mùirn beatha dàn.* Moments later I heard his voice as he greeted Jenna. All my nerve cells came alive at the sound and at the memory of yesterday, in his room.

"Does anyone want tea, or water, or a soda?" Matt offered as Cal came into the room, holding a big, beat-up leather satchel. "We don't keep alcohol in the house 'cause my dad's in AA."

This frank admission startled me. "Water sounds great." I crossed to Cal and gave him a quick kiss, marveling at my own boldness.

The doorbell rang again. A moment later Matt came back

into the room, carrying some bottles of seltzer. Robbie was right behind him. "Hey," he said.

I stared. I guess I should have been used to it by now, but I wasn't. It was as if Robbie's personality and lame social skills had been transferred into the body of a teen star. "Where are your glasses?" I asked.

Robbie took a bottle of seltzer from Matt and popped the cap. "That's the funny thing," he said slowly. "I don't need them anymore."

"How could you not need glasses?" I demanded. "Did you have laser surgery without telling me?"

"Nope," Robbie said. "That's what all the tests this week were about. Apparently my eyesight has just gotten better. I was having headaches because I didn't need to wear glasses anymore, and the lenses were straining my eyes."

He didn't sound happy, and it took me a few moments to realize that slowly, everyone's attention had turned to me.

"No!" I said strongly. "I absolutely did not do another spell! Honestly—I swear! I promised Robbie, and everyone else, that I wouldn't do another spell, and I haven't! I haven't done any spells at all!"

Robbie looked at me with his clear, gray-blue eyes, no longer hidden by thick, distorting lenses. "Morgan," he said.

"I swear! I absolutely promise you," I said, holding up my right hand. Robbie looked unconvinced. "Robbie! Believe me."

Conflict showed in his face. "What could it be, then?" he asked. "Eyes don't just get better. I mean, the actual shape of my eyeballs has changed. They were giving me MRIs to see if I had a tumor pressing on my brain."

"Jesus," Matt muttered.

"I don't know," I said helplessly. "But it wasn't me."

"This is incredible," said Jenna, sounding short of breath. "Could someone else have put a spell on him?"

"I could have," Cal said thoughtfully. "But I didn't. Morgan, do you remember the actual words of your spell?"

"Yes," I said. "But I put the spell on the potion I gave him, not on him."

"That's true," Cal mused. "Though if the potion was supposed to act on him in some way . . . what were the words?"

I swallowed, thinking back. "Um, 'So beauty in is beauty out," I recited softly. "This potion make your blemish nowt. This healing water makes you pure, and thus your beauty will endure."

"That was it?" Sharon asked. "God, why didn't you do it sooner?"

"Sharon," Robbie said in irritation.

"Okay, okay," said Cal. "We have a couple of possibilities here. One is that Robbie's eyes have spontaneously healed themselves due to some unfathomable miracle."

Ethan snorted, and Sharon shot him a glance.

"The second possibility," Cal went on, "is that Morgan's spell wasn't specific enough, wasn't limited only to Robbie's skin. It was a spell to eliminate blemishes, imperfections. His eyes were imperfect; now they're perfect. Like his skin."

The enormity of that thought was just sinking in when Ethan said brightly, "Great! I can't wait to see what it does for his personality!"

Jenna couldn't help snickering. I sank weakly into a chair shaped like a giant cupped hand.

"The third possibility," said Cal, "is that someone we

don't know has put a spell on Robbie. That doesn't seem likely—why would a stranger want to do that? No, I think it's more likely that Morgan's spell has just continued to fix things."

"That's kind of frightening," I said, chilled. Did I really have that kind of power?

"It's pretty unusual. That's why you're not supposed to be doing spells until you know more," Cal said. I felt terrible. "When we start learning spells, I'll show you how to limit them. Limitations are just about the most important things to know, along with how to channel power. When you work a spell, you need to limit it in time, effect, purpose, duration, and target."

"Oh, no." I dropped my head into my hands. "I didn't do any of that."

"And actually, now that I think about it, you banished limitations at the very first circle. Remember?" Cal asked. "That might have something to do with this also."

"So what now?" Robbie demanded. "What else is going to change?"

"Probably not much more," Cal said. "For one thing, even though Morgan's really powerful, she's still just a beginner. She's not in touch with her full powers."

I was glad he hadn't referred to me again as a blood witch. I wanted people to forget about it for now.

"Also," Cal said, "this kind of spell is usually self-limiting. I mean, the potion was for your face, and you put it only on your face, right? You didn't drink it or anything?"

"God, no," Robbie said.

Cal shrugged. "So it's just fixing that general area, including your eyes. It's unusual, but I guess it's not impossible."

"I don't believe this." I moaned, hiding my face. "I'm such an idiot. I can't believe I did this. I am so, so sorry, Robbie."

"What are you sorry about?" Ethan asked. "Now he can be an airline pilot."

Sharon giggled, then stifled it.

"So you don't think it's going to do anything else?" Robbie asked Cal.

"I don't know," Cal said. He grinned. "Have you been feeling especially smart lately? It could be working on your brain."

I moaned again.

Cal nudged me. "I'm only kidding. It's probably over. Stop worrying."

He clapped once. "Well. I think it's time to start talking about spells and limitations!"

I couldn't laugh, though some of the others did.

"This is our first circle without Bree, Raven, and Beth," said Cal.

"I'm going to miss them," said Jenna softly. Her eyes flicked to me, and I wondered if she thought it was my fault that they had left.

Cal nodded. "Yeah. Me too. But maybe without them we'll be more tightly focused. We'll find out."

We sat in a ring on the floor around Cal. "First, let's go over clans," he said. "You know how they all have qualities associated with them. The Brightendales were healers. The Woodbanes—the 'dark clan'—supposedly fought for power at any cost."

"Ooh," Robbie said. He gave me a mock-fearful look. But

I just shivered. The very idea of the Woodbanes made me cold. I didn't think it was something to laugh at.

"The Burnhides were known for their magick with crystals and gems," Cal went on. "The Leapvaughns were mischief makers. The Vikroths were warriors. And so on." He looked around the circle. "Well, just as each clan had qualities associated with it, so each clan also had certain runes that it tended to use. So—I think it's time we took a look at some runes."

Cal opened his large leather satchel and pulled out a sheaf of what looked like index cards. He held them up, and I saw that each one had a rune drawn on it, very large.

"Rune flash cards!" I said, and Cal nodded.

"Basically, yes," he said. "Using runes is a quick way to get in touch with a deep, old source of power. Tonight I just want to show them to you and have you concentrate on each one. Each symbol has many meanings. They're all there for you, if you open yourself up to them."

We all watched, fascinated, as he held up the white cards one by one, reading the runes' names and telling us what they traditionally stood for.

"There are different names for each symbol. The names depend on whether you're working within a Norse tradition, or German, or Gaelic," Cal explained. "Later on, we'll talk about which runes are associated with which clans."

"This is so beautiful," said Sharon. "I love that people have used these for thousands of years."

Ethan turned to her, nodding his agreement. I watched as their eyes met and held.

Who would have known that Sharon Goodfine would

find Wicca beautiful? Or that Ethan would dare to like her? Witchcraft was revealing us not only to ourselves but to each other.

"Let's make a circle," said Cal.

# 13

# Starlight

March 17, 1982

St. Paddy's day in New York City. Below, the city is celebrating a holiday they imported from my home, but I cannot join in. Angus is out looking for work. I sit here by the window, crying, though the Goddess knows I have no more tears left.

Everything I knew and loved is gone. My village is burned to the ground. My ma and da are dead, though it's still hard for me to believe it. My little cat Dagda. My friends. Belwicket has been wiped out, our cauldrons broken, our brooms burned, our herbs turned to smoke above our heads.

How did this happen? Why didn't I fall victim as so many others did? Why did Angus and I alone survive?

I hate New York, hate everything about it. The noise blunts my ears. I can't smell any living thing. I can't smell the sea or hear it in the background like a lullaby. There are people every-

*where, packed in tight, like sardines. The city is filthy; the people are rude and common. I ache for my home.*

*There is no magick in this place.*

*And yet if there is no magick, surely there is no true evil, either? — M. R.*

We purified our circle with salt and then invoked earth, air, water, and fire with a bowl of salt, a stick of incense, a bowl of water, and a candle. Cal showed us the rune symbols for these elements, and we worked to memorize them.

"Let's try to raise some energy and focus it," said Cal. "We'll try to focus it in ourselves, and we'll limit its effects to a good night's sleep and general well-being. And does anyone have any particular problem they'd like help with?" He met my eyes, and I could tell we were both thinking of my parents. But Cal left it up to me to ask for help in front of everyone, and I said nothing.

"Like, help my stepsister quit being such a pain?" Sharon asked. I hadn't known she had a stepsister. I was between Jenna and Sharon, and their hands felt small and smooth in mine.

Cal laughed. "You can't ask to change others. But you *could* ask to make it easier for *you* to get along with *her*."

"My asthma's been acting up since it got colder," Jenna said. I remembered her coughing but hadn't known she had asthma. People like Jenna, Sharon, Bree—they ruled our school. I had never really considered that they might have problems and difficulties. Not until Wicca came into all our lives.

"Okay, Jenna's asthma," agreed Cal. "Anything else?"

None of us said anything.

Cal lowered his head and closed his eyes, and we did the same. The room was filled with our deep, even breathing, and little by little, as the minutes passed, I felt our breathing tune in to one another, becoming aligned so that we inhaled and exhaled together.

Then Cal's voice, rich and slightly rough, said:

"Blessed be the animals, the plants, and all living things.
Blessed be the earth, the sky, the clouds, the rain.
Blessed be all people,
those within Wicca and those without.
Blessed be the Goddess and the God,
and all the spirits who help us.
Blessed be. We raise our hearts,
our voices, our spirits to the Goddess and the God."

As we began to move deasil, the words rose and fell in a pattern so that it became a song. We half skipped, half danced in our circle, and the chant became a joyous cry that filled the room, filled all the air around us. I was laughing, breathless, feeling happy and weightless and safe in this circle. Ethan was smiling but intent, his face flushed and his corkscrew curls bouncing around his head. Sharon's silky black hair was flying, and she looked pretty and carefree. Jenna looked like a blond fairy queen, and Matt was dark and purposeful. Robbie moved with new grace and coordination as we spun faster and faster. The only thing I missed was Bree's face in the circle.

I felt the energy rise. It coiled around us, building and

thickening and swirling in our circle. The living room floor was warm and smooth beneath my socked feet, and I felt like if I let go of Jenna's and Sharon's hands, I would fly off through the ceiling into the sky. As I looked above me, still chanting the words, I saw the white ceiling waver and dissolve to show me the deep indigo night and the white and yellow stars popping out of the sky so brightly. Awestruck, I gazed upward, seeing the infinite possibilities of the universe where before there had been only a ceiling. I wanted to reach out and touch the stars, and without hesitating, I unclasped my hands and stretched my arms overhead.

At the same instant everyone else let go and threw their arms overhead, and the circle stopped where it was while the swirling energy continued to coil around us, stronger and stronger. I reached for the stars, feeling the energy pressing against my backbone.

"Take the energy into you!" Cal called, and automatically I pressed my clasped fist against my chest. I breathed in warmth and white light and felt my worries melt away. I swayed on my feet and once again tried to touch the stars. Reaching overhead, I felt myself brush a tiny, prickly firelight that was hot and sharp against my fingers. It felt like a star, and I brought down my hand.

With the light in my hand I gazed at the others, wondering if they could see it. Then Cal was at my side because I always channeled too much energy and had to ground myself afterward. But this time I felt fine—not too dizzy, not too sick, just happy and lighthearted and full of wonder.

"Whoa," Ethan whispered, his eyes on me.

"What is that?" asked Sharon.

"Morgan!" Jenna said in awe. Her breath sounded tight and strained, and she was breathing fast and shallowly. I turned to her. I felt like I could do anything.

Reaching out, I pressed the light against her chest. She gasped with a small "Ah!" and I traced a line from one side to the other beneath her collarbones. Closing my eyes, I flattened my hand on her breastbone and felt the starlight dissolve into her. She gasped again and staggered on her feet, and Cal put out his hand but didn't touch me. Under my fingers I felt Jenna's lungs swell as she sucked in air. I felt the microscopic alveoli opening to admit oxygen, tiny capillaries absorbing the oxygen; I felt it as, from the smallest veins to the thick, ridged muscles of her bronchial tubes, each one expanded in a domino effect, loosening, relaxing, absorbing oxygen.

Jenna panted.

My eyes opened, and I smiled.

"I can breathe," Jenna said slowly, touching her chest. "I was starting to tighten up. I knew I'd need my inhaler after the circle, and I didn't want to use it in front of everyone." Jenna's eyes sought Matt, and he came to put his arm around her. "She opened up my lungs and put air in with that light," Jenna said, sounding dazed.

"Okay, stop," Cal said, gently taking my hands. "Quit touching things. Like on Samhain, maybe you should lie down and ground yourself."

I shook off his hands. "I don't want to ground myself," I said clearly. "I want to keep it." I flexed my fingers, wanting to touch something else, see what happened.

Cal looked at me. Something flickered in his eyes.

"I just want to keep this feeling," I explained.

"It can't stay forever," he said. "Energy doesn't linger—it needs to go somewhere. You don't want to go around zapping things."

I laughed. "I don't?"

"No," he assured me. Then he led me to a clear place on the polished wood floor, and I lay down, feeling the strength of the earth beneath my back, feeling the energy cease its whizzing around inside me, being absorbed by the earth's ancient embrace. In a few minutes I felt much more normal, less light-headed and . . . I guess, less drunk. Or at least, that's what I imagined feeling drunk was like. I didn't have much practice with it.

"Why can she do this?" Matt asked, his arm still protectively around Jenna. Jenna was taking deep, experimental breaths. "It's so easy," she marveled. "I feel so . . . so unconstricted."

Cal gave a wry chuckle. "It freaks me out, too, sometimes. Morgan does things that would be amazing for a high priestess to do—someone with years and years of training and experience. She just has a lot of power, that's all."

"You called her a blood witch," Ethan remembered. "She's a blood witch, like you. But how is that?"

"I don't want to talk about it," I said, sitting up. "I'm sorry if I did something I shouldn't have—again. But I didn't mean to do anything wrong. I just wanted to fix Jenna's breathing. I don't want to talk about being a blood witch. Okay?"

Six pairs of eyes looked at me. The members of my coven nodded or said okay. Only in Cal's face did I read the message that we would definitely have to talk about it later.

"I'm hungry," complained Ethan. "Got any munchies?"

"Sure," said Matt, heading toward the kitchen.

"Too bad we can't go swimming again," Jenna said regretfully.

"We can't?" Cal asked with a wicked smile at me. "Why not? My house isn't that far away."

Cringing, I crossed my arms over my chest.

"No way," Sharon scoffed, to my relief. "Even if the water is heated, the air's way too cold. I don't want to freeze."

"Oh, well," Cal said. Matt came in with a bowl of popcorn, and he helped himself to a big fistful. "Maybe some other time."

When no one could see me, I made a face at him, and he laughed silently.

I leaned against him, feeling warm and happy. It had been an amazing, exhilarating circle, even without Bree.

My smile faded as I wondered where she and Raven were tonight and who they were with.

# 14

# Lesson

May 7, 1982

We're leaving this soulless place. I've been working as a cashier in a diner, and Angus has been down in the meat district, unloading huge American cows and putting their carcasses on hooks. I feel my soul dying, and so does Angus. We're saving every penny so we can leave, go anywhere else.

Not much news from home. None of Belwicket is left to tell us what happened, and what little bits and pieces we get aren't enough to figure out anything. I don't even know why I write in this book anymore, except as a diary. It is no longer a Book of Shadows. It hasn't been since my birthday, when my world was destroyed. I haven't done any magick since being here, nor has Angus. No more will I. It has done nothing but wreak destruction.

I am only twenty, and yet I feel ready for death's embrace.

— M. R.

The next morning during church I suddenly had an idea. I glanced over at the dark confessionals. After the service was over, I told my parents that I wanted to make confession. They looked a little surprised, but what could they say?

"I don't want to go to the diner today," I added. "I'll just see you at home later."

Mom and Dad looked at each other, then Dad nodded.

Mom put her hand on my shoulder. "Morgan—," she began, then shook her head. "Nothing. I'll see you later, at home."

Mary K. looked at me but didn't say anything. Her face was troubled as she left with my parents.

I waited impatiently in line as parishioners went in to confess their sins. I realized I could probably tune in to what they were talking about, but I didn't want to try. It would be wrong. Father Hotchkiss heard some pretty steamy stuff sometimes, I'd guess. And probably some really boring, petty things, too.

Finally it was my turn. I knelt inside the cubicle and waited for the small grated window to slide open. When it did, I crossed myself and said, "Forgive me, Father, for I have sinned. It's been, um . . ." I thought back quickly. "Four months since my last confession."

"Go ahead, my child," said Father Hotchkiss, as he had all my life, every time I had confessed.

"Um . . ." I hadn't thought ahead this far and didn't have a list of sins ready. I really didn't want to go into some of the things I'd been doing, and I didn't consider them sins, anyway. "Well, lately I've been feeling very angry at my parents," I stated baldly. "I mean, I love my parents, and I try to honor them, but I recently . . . found out I was adopted." There. I had said it, and on the other side of the screen I saw Father Hotchkiss's head come up a bit as he took in my words. "I'm upset and angry that they didn't tell me before and that they won't talk to me about it now," I went on. "I want to know more about my birth parents. I want to know where I came from."

There was a long pause as Father Hotchkiss digested what I had said. "Your parents have done as they thought best," he said at last. He didn't deny that I was adopted, and I still felt humiliated that practically everyone had known but me.

"My birth mother is dead," I said, pushing on. I swallowed, feeling uncomfortable, even nervous talking about this. "I want to know more about her."

"My child," Father Hotchkiss said gently. "I understand your wishes. I can't say that I would not feel the same, were I in your place. But I tell you, and I speak with years of experience, that sometimes it really is best to leave the past alone."

Tears stung my eyes, but I hadn't really expected anything else. "I see," I whispered, trying not to cry.

"My dear, the Lord works in mysterious ways," said the priest, and I couldn't believe he was saying something so clichéd. He went on. "For some reason, God brought you to your parents, and I know they couldn't love you more. He chose them for you, and He chose you for them. It would be wise to respect His decision."

I sat and pondered this, wondering how true it was. Then I became aware that other people were waiting after me and it was time to go. "Thank you, Father," I said.

"Pray for guidance, my dear. And I will pray for you."

"Okay." I slipped out of the confessional, put on my coat, and headed out the huge double doors into bright November sunshine. I had to think.

After so many gray days it was nice to be walking in sunlight, kicking through the damp, brown leaves underfoot. Every now and then a golden leaf floated down around me, and each one that fell was like another second ticking off on the clock that turned autumn to winter.

I passed through downtown Widow's Vale, glancing in the shop windows. Our town is old, with the town hall dating back to 1692. Every once in a while I notice again how charming it is, how picturesque. A cool breeze lifted my hair, and I caught a scent of the Hudson River, bordering the town.

By the time I got home, I'd thought about what Father Hotchkiss had said. I could see some wisdom in his words, but that didn't mean I could accept not knowing the whole truth. I didn't know what to do. Maybe I would ask for guidance at the next circle.

Walking two miles had warmed me up nicely, and I tossed my jacket over a chair in the kitchen. I glanced at the clock. If I assumed my family followed their usual routine at the diner, they wouldn't be home for another hour or so. It would be nice to have the house to myself for a while.

A thump overhead made me freeze. Weirdly, the first thought I had was that Bree was in my house, possibly with Raven, and they were casting a spell on my bedroom or something. I don't know why I didn't think of burglars or a stray squirrel that had somehow gotten in—I just immediately thought of Bree.

I heard scuffling sounds and the loud scraping noise of a piece of furniture being jolted out of place. I quietly opened the mudroom door and picked up my baseball bat. Then I kicked off my shoes and headed upstairs in my stocking feet.

By the time I reached the top of the landing, I could tell the sounds were coming from Mary K.'s room. Then I heard her voice, saying, "Ow! Stop it! Dammit, Bakker!"

I stopped, unsure of what to do.

"Get off me," Mary K. said angrily.

"Oh, come on, Mary K.," was Bakker's response. "You said you loved me! I thought that meant—"

"I told you I didn't want to do that!" Mary K. cried.

I flung open the door to find Bakker Blackburn entangled with my sister on her single bed. Her legs were kicking.

"Hey!" I said loudly, making them both jump. Their heads turned to stare at me, and I saw relief in Mary K.'s eyes. "You heard her," I said loudly. "Get off!"

"We're just talking," said Bakker.

Mary K.'s hands pushed against his chest, and he resisted it. Fury roiled inside me, and I raised the bat.

Whap! I gave Bakker a smart rap on his shoulder to get his attention. I hadn't been this furious since Bree and I'd had our last fight.

"Ow!" Bakker yelled. "What are you doing? Are you nuts?"

"Bakker, get off!" Mary K. said again, pushing at him.

I thrust my face close to Bakker's, and with my teeth clenched, I spoke as menacingly as I could. "Get the hell off her!"

Bakker's face went stiff, and he quickly moved away from the bed. He looked embarrassed and angry, his eyes dark.

Then he snapped out his hand and knocked the bat out of my grip. My jaw dropped in surprise as the wood went flying across the room.

"Stay out of this, Morgan," he said. "You don't know what's going on. Mary K. and I are just talking."

"Ha!" said Mary K., jumping up from the bed and yanking down her shirt. "You're being an ass! Now get out!"

"Not until you tell me what's going on," Bakker said. "You said come over!" He was almost yelling, his voice filling the room. "You said come up here! What was I supposed to think? We've been going out almost two months!"

Mary K. was crying now. "I didn't mean that," she said, holding her pillow to her stomach. "I just wanted to be alone with you."

"What did you think being alone with me was all about?" he asked, his arms wide. He took a step closer to her.

"Watch it, Bakker," I warned, but he ignored me.

"I didn't mean that," Mary K. repeated, crying.

"Jesus!" he said, leaning over her. My teeth clenched, and I started edging over toward the bat. "You don't know what you want."

"Shut up, Bakker," I snapped. "For God's sake, she's fourteen."

Mary K. cried into her pillow.

"She's my girlfriend!" Bakker shouted. "I love her, and she loves me, so stay out of this! It's none of your business!"

"None of my business?" I couldn't believe what I was hearing. "That's my little sister you're talking about!"

Without planning it, I snapped out my arm, finger pointed at Bakker. Before my eyes a small ball of spitting, crackly blue light shot out of my finger and streaked toward him, hitting him in the side. It was like the light I had given to Jenna last night, but different. Bakker yelped and stumbled, clutching his side and clawing at the bedspread. I stared at him, horrified, and he stared back at me as if I had suddenly sprouted wings and claws.

"What the hell—" he gasped, clasping his side. I was praying blood wouldn't start running out through his fingers. When he took his hand away, there were no marks on his shirt, no blood. I breathed out in relief.

"I'm out of here," he said in a strangled voice, lurching to his feet. He turned back to look at Mary K. one last time. She had her face buried in her pillow, and she didn't look up. With a last glare at me Bakker stormed through the bedroom door and pounded down the steps. The front door slammed moments later, and I peeked out down the stairwell to make sure he was gone. Through the front door sidelight I saw him striding fast down the street, rubbing his side. His lips were moving as if he was swearing to himself.

Back in Mary K.'s room, she was holding a tissue to her eyes and sniffling.

"Jesus, Mary K.," I said, sitting next to her on the bed. "What was that about? Why aren't you at the diner?"

She started crying again and leaned forward into me. I put my arms around her and held her, so thankful she hadn't been hurt, that I had come home when I had. For the first time in a week it felt like the two of us again, the way we used to be. Close. Comfortable. Trusting each other. I had missed that so much.

"Don't tell Mom and Dad," she said, tears wetting her cheeks. "I just wanted to see Bakker alone, so I told them I needed to study, and I had them drop me off here while they went to lunch. It's just—we're always with other people. I didn't know he would think—"

"Oh, Mary K.," I said, trying to soothe her. "It was a huge misunderstanding, but it wasn't your fault. Just because you said you wanted to see him alone doesn't mean that you're obligated to go to bed with him. You meant one thing; he understood another. What's awful is what an ass he was being. I should have called the cops."

Mary K. sniffled and drew back. "I don't really think he was going to . . . hurt me," she said. "I think it kind of looked worse than it was."

"I can't believe you're defending him!"

"I'm not," said my sister. "I'm not defending him, and I'm definitely breaking up with him."

"Good," I said strongly.

"But I have to say, it really wasn't like him," Mary K. went on. "He's never pushed me too far, always listened when I said no. I'm sure he'll be really sorry tomorrow."

My eyes narrowed as I looked at her. "Mary Kathleen Rowlands, that's not good enough. Don't you dare make excuses for him. When I walked in here, he was pinning you down!"

Her brows creased. "Yeah," she said.

"And he knocked the bat out of my hands," I said. "And he was yelling at us."

"I know," said Mary K., looking angry. "I can't believe him."

"That's more like it," I said, standing up. "Tell me you're breaking up with him."

"I'm breaking up with him," my sister repeated.

"Okay. Now I'm going to go change. You better wash

your face and straighten your room before Mom and Dad come home."

"Okay," said Mary K., standing up. She gave me a watery smile. "Thanks for rescuing me." She reached out to hug me.

"You're welcome," I said, and turned to go.

"How did you stop him, anyway? He said, 'Ow!' and then fell against the bed. What did you do?"

I thought fast. "I kicked his knee and made it buckle," I said. "Made him lose his balance."

Mary K. laughed. "I bet he was surprised."

"I think we both were," I said honestly. Then, feeling a little shaky, I went downstairs. I had shot a bolt of light at someone. Surely that was strange, even for a witch.

# 15

# Who I Am

September 1, 1982

Today we're moving out of this hellhole, to a town about three hours north of here. It's called Meshomah Falls. I think Meshomah is an Indian word. They have Indian words all over the place around here. The town is small and very pretty, kind of like home.

We already have jobs — I'm going to waitress at the little café in town, and Angus will be helping a local carpenter. We saw people dressed in queer old-fashioned clothes there last week. I asked a local man about them, and he said they were Amish.

Last week Angus got back from Ireland. I didn't want him to go, and I couldn't write about it until now. He went to Ireland, and he went to Ballynigel. Not much of the town is left. Every house where a witch lived was burned to the ground and now has been razed flat for rebuilding. He said none of our kind are left there, none he could find. Over in Much Bencham he got a story that people have been telling about a huge dark wave that wiped out the town, a wave without water. I don't know what could cause or create something so big, so powerful. Maybe many covens working together.

I was terrified for him to go, thought I'd never see him again. He wanted to get married before he left, and I said no. I can't marry anyone. Nothing is permanent, and I don't want to fool myself. Anyway, he took the money, went home, and found a bunch of charred, empty fields.

Now he's here, and we're moving, and in this new town, I'm hoping a new life can begin. —M. R.

Late that afternoon I decided to hunt down my Wicca books. I lay on my bed and cast out my senses, sort of feeling my way through the whole house. For a long time I got nothing, and I started to think I was wasting my time. But then, after about forty-five minutes, I realized I felt the books in my mom's closet, inside a suitcase at the very back. I looked, and sure enough, there they were. I took them back to my room and put them on my desk. If Mom or Dad wanted to make something of it, let them. I was through with silence.

On Sunday night I was sitting at my desk, working my way through math homework, when my parents knocked on my door.

"Come in," I said.

The door opened, and I heard Mary K.'s music playing louder from inside her room. I winced. Our musical tastes are completely different.

I saw my parents standing in the doorway. "Yes?" I said coolly.

"May we come in?" Mom asked.

I shrugged.

Mom and Dad came in and sat down on my bed. I tried not to glance at the Wicca books on my desk.

Dad cleared his throat, and Mom took his hand.

"This past week has been very . . . difficult for all of us," Mom said, looking reluctant and uncomfortable. "You've had questions, and we weren't ready to answer them."

I waited.

She sighed. "If you hadn't found out on your own, I probably never would have wanted to tell you about the adoption," she said, her voice ending on a whisper. "I know that's not what people recommend. They say everyone should be open, honest." She shook her head. "But telling you didn't seem like a good idea." She raised her eyes to my dad's, and he nodded at her.

"Now you know about it," Mom said. "Part of it, anyway. Maybe it's best for you to know as much as we know. I'm not sure. I'm not sure what the best thing is anymore. But we don't seem to have a choice."

"I have a right to know," I said. "It's my life. It's all I can think about. It's there, every day."

Mom nodded. "Yes, I see that. So." She drew in a long breath and looked down at her lap for a moment. "You know Daddy and I got married when I was twenty-two and he was twenty-four."

"Uh-huh."

"We wanted to start a family right away," said my mom. "We tried for eight years, with no luck. The doctors found one thing wrong with me after another. Hormonal imbalances, endometriosis . . . it got to where every month I would get my period and cry for three days because I wasn't pregnant."

My dad kept his gaze on her. He freed his hand from hers and wrapped his arm around her shoulders instead.

"I was praying to God to send me a baby," said Mom. "I lit candles, said novenas. Finally we applied at an adoption agency, and they told us it might be three or four years. But we applied anyway. Then . . ."

"Then an acquaintance of ours, a lawyer, called us one night," said my dad.

"It was raining," my mom put in as I thought about their friends, trying to remember a lawyer.

"He said he had a baby," my dad said. He shifted and tucked his hands under his knees. "A baby girl who needed adopting, a private adoption."

"We didn't even think about it," Mom said. "We just said yes! And he came over that night with a baby and handed her to me. And I took one look and knew this was *my* baby, the one I'd prayed for for so long." Mom's voice broke, and she rubbed her eyes.

"That was you," Dad said unnecessarily. He smiled at the memory. "You were seven months old and just so—"

"So perfect," Mom interrupted, her face lighting up. "You were plump and healthy, with curly hair and big eyes, and you looked up at me . . . and I knew you were the one. In that moment you became my child, and I would have killed anyone who tried to take you away from me. The lawyer said that your birth parents were too young to raise a baby and had asked him to find you a good home." She shook her head, remembering. "We didn't even think about it, didn't ask for more information. All I knew was, I had my baby, and frankly, I didn't care where you had come from or why."

I clenched my jaw, feeling my throat start aching. Had my birth parents given me to someone to keep me safe, knowing they were in danger somehow? Had the lawyer been telling the truth? Or had I just been found somewhere, after they were dead?

"You were everything we wanted," said Dad. "That night you slept between us in our bed, and the next day we went out and bought every kind of baby thing we'd ever heard of. It was like a thousand Christmases, all of our dreams coming true, in you."

"A week later," Mom said, sniffling, "we read about a fire in Meshomah Falls. How two bodies had been found in a barn that had burned to the ground. When the bodies were identified, they matched the names on your birth certificate."

"We wanted to know more, but we also didn't want to do anything to hurt the adoption," said my dad. He shook his head. "I'm ashamed to say, we just wanted to keep you, no matter what."

"But months later, after the adoption was final—it went through really fast, and finally it was all legal and no one could take you away—then we tried to find out more," Mom continued.

"How?" I asked.

"We tried calling the lawyer, but he had taken a job in another state. We left messages, but he never returned any of our calls. It was kind of odd," Dad added. "It almost seemed like he was avoiding us. Finally we gave up on him.

"I went through the newspapers," Dad went on. "I talked to the reporter who had covered the fire story, and he put me in touch with the Meshomah police. And after that I did research in Ireland, when I was there on a business trip. That was when you were about two years old and your mom was expecting Mary K."

"What did you find out?" I asked in a small voice.

"Are you sure you want to know?"

I nodded, gripping my desk chair. "I do want to know," I said, my voice stronger. I knew what Alyce had told me and what I had found out at the library. I needed to know more. I needed to know it all.

"Maeve Riordan and Angus Bramson died in that barn fire," my dad said, looking down as if he were reading the words off his shoes. "It was arson—murder," he clarified. "The barn doors had been locked from the outside, and gasoline had been poured around the building."

I trembled, my eyes huge and fastened on my dad. I hadn't read anywhere that it had definitely been murder.

"They found symbols on some of the charred pieces of wood," said Mom. "They were identified as runes, but no one knew why they were written there or why Maeve and Angus had been killed. They had kept to themselves, had no debts, went to church on Sundays. The crime was never solved."

"What about in Ireland?"

Dad nodded and shifted his weight. "Like I said, I went there on business, and I didn't have a lot of time. I didn't even know what to look for. But I took a day trip to the town where the Meshomah police had said Maeve Riordan was from: Ballynigel. When I got there, there wasn't much of a town to see. A couple of shops on a main street and one or two ugly new apartment buildings. My guidebook had said it was a quaint old fishing village, but there was hardly any sign of it or what it had used to be."

"Did you find out what happened?"

"Not really," Dad said, holding his hands wide. "There was a newsstand there, a little shop. When I asked about it, the old lady kicked me out and slammed the door."

"Kicked you out?" I asked in amazement.

Dad gave a dry chuckle. "Yes. Finally, after walking around and finding nothing, I went to the next town—I think its name was Much Bencham—and had lunch in the pub. There were a couple of old guys sitting at the bar, and they struck up a conversation with me, asking where I was from. I started talking, but as soon as I mentioned Ballynigel they went quiet. 'Why do ye want to know?' they asked suspiciously. I said I was investigating a story for my hometown newspaper about small Irish towns. For the travel section."

I stared at my dad, unable to picture him blithely lying to strangers, going on this quest to find out my heritage. He'd known all of this, both of them had, almost all of my life. And they'd never breathed a word to me.

"To make a long story short," Dad went on, "it finally came out that until four years earlier, Ballynigel *had* been a small, prosperous town. But in 1982 it had suddenly been destroyed. Destroyed by evil, they said."

I could hardly breathe. This was similar to what Alyce had said. My mom was chewing her bottom lip nervously, not looking at me.

"They said that Ballynigel had been a town of witches, with most of the people there being descendants of witches for thousands of years. They called them the old clans. They said evil had risen up and destroyed the witches, and they didn't know why, but they knew you should never take a chance with a witch." Dad coughed and cleared his throat. "I laughed and said I didn't believe in witches. And they said, 'More fool you.' They said that witches were real and there had been a powerful coven at Ballynigel until the night they had been destroyed, and the whole town with them. Then I had an idea, and I asked, Did anyone escape? They said a few humans. Humans, they called them, as if there was a difference. I said, What about witches? And they shook their heads and said if any witches had escaped, they would never be safe, no matter where they went. That they would be hunted down and killed, if not sooner, then later."

But two witches had escaped and had come to America. Where they were killed three years later.

Mom had quit sniffling and now watched my dad as if she hadn't heard this story for many years.

"I came home and told your mom about it, and to tell you the truth, we were both pretty frightened. We thought about how your birth parents had been killed. Frankly, it scared us. We thought there was a psycho out there, hunting these people down, and if he knew about you, you wouldn't be safe. So we decided to go on with our business, and we never spoke of your past again."

I sat there, interlacing this story with the one Alyce had told me. For the first time I could almost understand why my parents had kept all this to themselves. They had been trying to protect me. Protect me from what had killed my birth parents.

"We wanted to change your first name," Mom said. "But

you were legally Morgan. So we gave you a nickname."

"Molly," I said, light dawning. I had been Molly until fourth grade, when I decided I hated it and wanted to be called Morgan.

"Yes. And by then, when you wanted to be Morgan again, well, we felt safe," Mom said. "So much had changed. We'd never heard anything more about Meshomah Falls or Ballynigel or witches. We thought all of that was behind us."

"Then we found your Wicca books," said Dad. "And it brought everything back, all the memories, the awful stories, the fear. I thought someone had found you, had given you those books for a reason."

I shook my head. "I bought them myself."

"Maybe we've been unreasonable," Mom said slowly. "But you don't know what it's like to worry that your child might be taken from you or might be harmed. Maybe what you're doing is innocent and the people you're doing it with don't mean any harm."

"Of course they don't," I said, thinking of Cal, and his mother, and my friends.

"But we can't help feeling afraid," said my dad. "I saw a whole town that had been wiped out. I read about the burned barn. I talked to those men in Ireland. If that's what witchcraft entails, we don't want you to have any part of it."

We sat there in silence for a few minutes while I tried to absorb this story. I felt overwhelmed with emotion, but most of my anger toward them had melted away.

"I don't know what to say." I took a deep breath. "I'm glad you told me all this. And maybe I wouldn't have understood it when I was younger. But I still think you should have told me about the adoption part earlier. I should have known."

My parents nodded, and my mom sighed heavily.

"But I can't help feeling that Wicca is not connected to that—disaster in Ireland. It's just—a weird coincidence. I mean, Wicca is a part of me. And I know I'm a witch. But the kind of stuff we do couldn't cause anything like what you described."

Mom looked like she wanted to ask more but didn't want to hear the answers. She kept silent.

"How come you were able to have Mary K.?" I asked.

"I don't know," Mom said in a low voice. "It just happened. And after Mary K., I've never gotten pregnant again. God wanted me to have two daughters, and you've both brought untold joy into our lives. I care about you both so much that I can't stand to think of any danger coming to you. Which is why I want you to leave witchcraft alone. I'm *begging* you to leave witchcraft alone."

She started crying, so of course I did, too. It was all too much to take in.

"But I can't!" I wailed, blowing my nose. "It's a part of me. It's natural. It's like having brown hair or big feet. It's just—me."

"You don't have big feet," my dad objected.

I couldn't help laughing through my tears.

"I know you love me and want what's best for me," I said, wiping my eyes. "And I love you and don't want to hurt you or disappoint you. But it's like you're asking me not to be Morgan anymore." I looked up.

"We want you to be safe!" my mom said strongly, meeting my eyes. "We want you to be happy."

"I'm happy," I said. "And I try to be safe all the time."

The music went off across the hall, and we heard Mary K. enter the bathroom that connected her room to mine. The water ran, and we heard her brushing her teeth. Then the door shut again and it was quiet.

I looked at my parents. "Thank you for telling me," I said. "I know it was hard, but I'm glad that you did. I needed to know. And I'll think about what you said, I promise."

Mom sighed, and she and my dad looked at each other. They stood, and we all hugged each other for the first time in a week.

"We love you," said Mom into my hair.

"I love you, too," I said.

# 16

# Hostile

December 15, 1982

We're getting ready to celebrate Christmas for the first time ever. We're going to the Catholic church in town. The people are very nice. It's funny, all the Christmas stuff—it's so close to Yule. The Yule log, the colors red and green, the mistletoe. Those things have always been a part of my life. It feels strange to be practicing Catholics instead of what we were.

This town is nice, much greener than New York City. I can see nature here; I can smell rain. It's not a bunch of ugly gray boxes full of unhappy people racing around.

Over and over I find myself wanting to say a little spell for this or that—to get rid of slugs in the garden, to bring more sunshine, to help my bread rise. But I don't. My whole life is in black and white, and that's the way it has to be now. No spells, no magick, no rituals, no rhymes. Not here. Not ever.

Anyway, I love our wee house. It's lovely and easy for me to keep clean. We're saving up to buy our own washing machine. Imagine! Everyone in America has their own.

I can't forget the horror of this year. It is seared on my soul forever. But I am glad to be in this new place, safe, with Angus.

—M. R.

"Are you going to the game on Friday?" Tamara asked me.

I kicked off my clogs and stowed them in the bottom of my gym locker. As usual, the air in the girls' locker room smelled like a mixture of sweat, baby powder, and shampoo. Tamara pulled on her gym shorts and sat down to put on her socks.

"I don't know," I answered, pulling my shirt over my head. Quickly I wriggled into my gym clothes and saw Tamara's eyes glance at the small silver pentacle around my neck. She looked away, and I wasn't sure if she got the significance: that it was a symbol of my commitment to Wicca and to Cal. I bent down to tie my sneakers and didn't say anything about it.

Across the room Bree stood next to her own locker, changing. Since Raven was a senior, she was in a different class. It was unusual to see Bree alone.

Bree's eyes met mine for a moment, and their coldness shocked me. It was hard to believe that I hadn't been able to share my huge news with her: finding out I was adopted, the story of my birth parents. We had always promised to tell each other everything, and until this school year we had. She'd told me about when she'd lost her virginity and tried pot for the first time and how she'd found out about her mom's affair. My own confidences had been much more banal.

"Guess who asked me out," said Tamara, pulling her tight curls into a puffy ponytail.

"Who?" I asked, quickly braiding my hair in two long braids so I looked like an Irish Pocahontas.

Tamara lowered her voice. "Chris Holly."

My eyes got wide. "Get out! What did you say?" I whispered.

"I said no! Number one, I'm sure he only asked because he's flunking trig and needs help, and number two, I saw what a jerk he was with Bree." Her dark brown eyes looked at me. "Are you two talking yet?"

I shook my head.

So did Tamara. I shoved my feet into my sneakers and tied them.

"So did you go after Cal?" she asked.

"No," I said honestly. "I mean, I was crazy about him, but I knew Bree liked him. I just assumed they'd end up together. But then . . . he picked me." Shrugging, I stuck my braids down the back of my T-shirt so they wouldn't whip anyone in the face. Then Ms. Lew, our PE teacher, blew her whistle. Ms. Lew loved that whistle.

"It's raining out, girls!" she called in her clear voice. "So give me five laps around the gym!"

We all groaned, as expected, then started to jog out of the locker room. Tamara and I quickly passed Bree, who was going as slowly as she possibly could.

"Witch," I heard Bree mutter as I jogged past. My cheeks burned, and I pretended not to hear her.

"She called you a bitch," Tamara whispered angrily, jogging next to me. "I can't believe she's being such a bad sport about this. I mean, they didn't even go out. Besides, she can get any *other* guy she wants. Does she really have to have them all?"

Hooting and whistling assaulted our ears as all the junior boys ran out of their locker room and started jogging in the opposite direction. I could hear the rain as it hit the small windows set high in the gym walls.

"Hey, baby!"

"Looking good!"

I rolled my eyes as the boys jogged past. Robbie made a face at me as he passed, and I laughed.

"Bree says they did go out once," I said, starting to pant. Actually, she had said that she and Cal had sex. It wasn't exactly the same thing.

Tamara shrugged. "Maybe they did, but I never heard about it. It couldn't have meant much, anyway. Oh, guess who asked Janice out? You've been out of the whole gossip loop."

"Who?"

"Ben Reggio," announced Tamara. "They've had two study dates."

"Oh, that's great," I said. "They seem like they'd be perfect together. I hope it works out."

I felt so normal, talking about regular high school stuff with Tamara. As exciting and fantastic and empowering as my Wicca experiences were, they made me feel kind of isolated. They were also exhausting. It was nice, not having to think about anything deep or life changing for a few minutes.

After our laps we split into teams for volleyball. The girls were on one side of the gym with Ms. Lew, and the boys were on the other with Coach.

Bree and I ended up on opposite teams.

"God, look at Robbie," a girl whispered behind me. I

turned around and saw Bettina Kretts talking to Paula Arroyo. "He is so hot."

I looked at Robbie. With great skin and no glasses, he was moving around the volleyball court with new confidence.

"I heard that senior, Anu Radtha, asked when he had transferred here," Paula said in a low voice.

I raised an eyebrow. Anu was the older sister of one of Bree's old boyfriends, Ranjit. So Anu actually thought Robbie was a new student and one worthy of a senior's attention.

"Is he going out with anyone?" Bettina asked.

"Don't think so," Paula answered. Their conversation was interrupted when the ball came into our quarter for a minute. We bounced it around, and I knocked it across the net, anxious to hear the rest of what they were saying.

"He hangs out with the witches," Bettina shocked me by saying. She was several people away and speaking in a low tone. Only by concentrating could I hear what she was saying. I'd had no idea that people around school thought of our group as "the witches."

"Yeah, I've seen him with Cal and the rest of them," said Paula. "Hey, if he isn't going out with anyone, why don't you ask him to the game?"

Bettina giggled. "Maybe I will."

Well, well, well, I thought, popping the ball over to Sarah Fields. She hit it over the net to Janice, and Janice returned with a quick, neat pop that went right between Bettina and Alessandra Spotford, costing us a point and giving our opponents the serve.

Bree was in the server's position on the other team, and while she was holding the ball, someone gave a wolf whistle from the other side of the gym. She looked up, her eyes flitting from boy to boy until she found Seth Moore giving her a big, lecherous grin. Seth was good-looking in a punky kind of way. His hair was cut in a buzzed flattop, he wore two silver earrings in his left ear, and he had pretty hazel eyes.

Bree grinned back and wiggled her shoulders at him.

Automatically I looked for Chris Holly, Bree's most recent ex. He was watching it all with a kind of frozen animosity, but he said nothing and made no move.

"Come on, Miss Warren," ordered Ms. Lew.

"You and me, baby!" Seth shouted.

Bree laughed, and then our glances met. She gave me this snarky, superior smile, as if to say, See? Boys would never do that for *you.* I tried to look bored, but of course it was true. Cal was the only guy who had ever paid me any attention. Bree's showing off hurt me, as she intended.

"Anytime!" Bree called to Seth, getting ready to serve. Several of his teammates made a big show of holding him back. Everyone was laughing now, everyone but me, Chris Holly—and one other person. When I saw the look on Robbie's face, my jaw almost dropped open. Good old Robbie, my pal Robbie, was watching Bree and Seth with a barely concealed jealousy. His hands were clenching at his sides, and his whole body was tense.

Huh, I thought in wonder. He had never said a word about liking Bree.

Then I felt a stab of guilt. Of course, I hadn't asked.

"Come on, Bree," said Ms. Lew, sounding irritated.

Bree gave me another superior smile, as if this whole show was for my benefit, to show me how hot she was and how nothing I was. A spark of anger ignited in me. Looking at her, I impulsively hooked my finger in the neck of my T-shirt and tugged it down, revealing the silver pentacle that Cal had once worn and that was now mine.

Bree paled visibly and drew in a quick breath. Then she pulled back her arm, made a fist, and smashed the volleyball right at me with all her strength. Automatically I threw my hand in front of my face a split second before the powerful serve came right at me. It knocked me down, and the entire junior class saw me whack my head on the wooden floor. A tangy, coppery smell alerted me one second before my nose and mouth filled with blood. Putting my hands over my face, I tried to sit up before I drowned, and my blood ran out through my fingers and down my shirt.

Everyone was gasping, talking fast, and Ms. Lew's voice, urgent and in control, said, "Let me see, honey." Her hands pried my fingers away from my face, and when she did, I saw Bree, standing over her, peering at me in alarm, a horrified expression on her face.

I looked at her, trying not to swallow blood. Her mouth opened, and silently she said, "I'm sorry." She looked so much like her old self for a minute that I almost felt happy. Then all of a sudden the shock subsided, and my face was filled with pain.

"Are you all right?" someone asked.

"Unh," I mumbled, putting my hands up to my nose. "Hurts."

"Okay, Morgan," said Ms. Lew. "Can you stand up? Let's get you to my office so we can put some ice on it. I think we'd better call your mom." She helped me up and called, "Get back to the game, girls. Bettina, get some paper towels and wipe that blood up so someone doesn't slip on it. Ms. Warren, see me in my office after class."

I cast a last look at Bree as I left. Bree looked back at me, but suddenly every remnant of friendship or emotion was gone, replaced by calculation. It made my heart sink, and tears filled my eyes.

When Mom came to get me, she was still in her work clothes. Clucking with worry, she took me to the emergency room, where they X-rayed my face. My nose was broken, and my lip needed one tiny stitch. Everything was swollen, and I looked like a Halloween mask.

It had come to this, between me and Bree.

# 17

# The New Coven

April 14, 1983

My peas are coming up nicely — I thought I might have put them in too early. They're a symbol of my new life: I can't believe they're growing on their own so strongly, without magickal help. Sometimes the urge to get in touch with the Goddess is so strong, I ache with it — it's like a pain, something trying to get out. But that part of my life is over, and all I have from that time is my name. And Angus.

We have a new addition to our household: a gray-and-white kitten. I've named her Bridget. She's a funny little thing, with extra toes on each paw and the biggest purr you ever heard. I'm glad to have her.

—M. R.

That afternoon, as I lay in bed with an ice pack on my face, the doorbell rang.

I immediately sensed that it was Cal. My heart thumped painfully. I listened as he spoke to my mom. I focused my attention, but I could still barely make out their words.

"Well, I don't know," I heard Mom say.

"For Pete's sake, Mom. I'll stay the whole time and chaperon them," said Mary K., much louder. She must have been standing right at the bottom of the steps. Then footsteps sounded on the stairs. I watched nervously as my door opened.

Mom came in first, presumably to make sure I was properly dressed and not, say, wearing a sexy, see-through negligee. In fact, I was wearing stretched-out gray sweatpants, an undershirt of my dad's, and a white sweatshirt. Mom had helped me wash the blood out of my hair, but I hadn't dried it or anything like that. It hung loose in long damp ropes. Basically, I looked as awful as I had ever looked in my life.

Cal came into my room, and his presence made it seem small and young. Note to self: Redecorate.

He gave me a big smile and said, "Darling!"

I couldn't help laughing, though it hurt, and I put my hand to my face and said, "Ungh—doan make me laugh."

As soon as Mom saw I was decent, she left, even though she was obviously uncomfortable about my having a boy in my room.

"Doesn't she look great?" Mary K. said. "Too bad Halloween's over. I bet by Thursday everything will be yellow and green." I noticed she was holding a white teddy bear wearing a heart-shaped bib.

"For me?" I asked.

Mary K. shook her head, looking embarrassed. "It's from Bakker."

I nodded. Bakker had been sending flowers and leaving notes on our porch all day. He'd called several times, and when I had answered the phone, he had apologized to me. I knew Mary K. was weakening.

She perched in my desk chair, and I gave her a look. "Don't you have homework?"

"I promised to chaperon," she objected. Then, seeing my expression, she held up her hands. "Okay, okay, I'm going."

As the door closed behind her I looked at Cal. "I didn't want you to see me like this." Because of the swelling in my nose, my voice sounded clogged and distant.

His face grew solemn. "Tamara told me about what happened. Do you think she did it on purpose?"

I thought of Bree's face, of the fright in her eyes when she saw what she'd done to me.

"It was an accident," I said, and he nodded.

"I brought you some stuff." He held up a small bag.

"What?" I asked eagerly.

"This, for starters," Cal said, taking out a small potted plant. It was silvery gray, with cut, feathery leaves.

"Artemesia," I said, recognizing it from one of my herb books. "It's pretty."

Cal nodded. "Mugwort. A useful plant. Also this." He handed me a small vial.

I read the label. "*Arnica montana.*"

"It's a homeopathic medicine," Cal explained. "I got it at the health-food store. It's for when you've had a traumatic injury. It's good for bruises, stuff like that." He leaned closer. "I spelled it to help you heal faster," he whispered. "It's just what the doctor ordered."

I sank back gratefully on my pillows. "Cool."

"One more thing," Cal said, taking out a bottle of Yoo-Hoo. "I bet you can't eat much, but a Yoo-Hoo can be sucked down with a straw. And it's got all the major food groups—dairy, fat, chocolate. You could say it's the perfect food."

I laughed, trying not to move my face. "Thanks. You thought of everything."

Mom called upstairs: "Dinner will be ready in five minutes."

I rolled my eyes, and Cal smiled. "I can take a hint," he said. He sat carefully on the edge of my bed and took my hand in both of his. I swallowed, feeling lost, wanting to hold him to me. *Mùirn beatha dàn*, I thought.

"Is there anything you want me to do for you?" he asked with quiet meaning. I knew he meant, Do you want me to get back at Bree?

I shook my head, feeling my face ache. "I don't think so," I whispered. "Let it go."

He regarded me evenly. "I'll let it go so far and no further," he warned. "This sucks."

I nodded, feeling very tired.

"Okay, I'll get going. Call me later if you want to talk."

He stood up. Then he very gently put his hands on my face, barely touching me with his fingertips. He closed his eyes and muttered words I didn't understand. Closing my eyes, I felt the heat from his fingers warm my face. As I breathed in, some of the pain dissipated.

It took less than a minute, then he opened his eyes and stepped back. I felt much better.

"Thanks," I said. "Thanks for coming."

"I'll talk to you later," he said. Then he turned and left my room.

As I sank back down in bed my face felt lighter, less

swollen. My head hurt less. I opened the arnica and popped four of the tiny sugar pills under my tongue. Then I lay quietly, feeling the pain wash out of me.

That night before I went to sleep, both my black eyes were almost gone, the swelling had gone way down, and I felt like I could breathe through my nose.

I stayed home from school the next day, although I looked tons better, except for the ugly black stitch on my lip.

At two-thirty that afternoon I called Mom at work and told her I was going over to Tamara's house to pick up some homework assignments.

"Are you sure you feel up to it?" she asked.

"Yeah, I feel almost fine," I said. "I'll be back before dinner."

"Okay, then. Drive carefully."

"I will."

I hung up the phone, got my keys and my coat, put on my clogs, and set off toward school. It's pretty much impossible to hide a huge white whale like Das Boot, but I parked on a side street two blocks away, where I thought I could see Bree's car pass as she left school. I could have waited for her at home, but I wasn't sure she'd go straight there.

It wasn't like I had a totally fleshed-out plan. Basically I was hoping to confront Bree, to hash everything out. In the best of all possible worlds, it would have a positive result. I felt like I had reached a breakthrough with my parents, and Mary K. and I had bonded again after the Bakker incident: Now I wanted to get things straight with Bree. The habits of a lifetime aren't easy to erase, and I still thought of her as my best friend. Hating her was too much to bear. The scene in gym showed how desperately we needed to work things out.

But it wasn't only that. I had other reasons for wanting to

mend things between us, too. Magick was clarity. According to my books, to work the best magick was to see the most clearly. If I lived with an ongoing feud in my life, it could seriously hamper my ability to do magick.

I almost missed Bree's car as it passed the corner at the end of the block. Quickly I started up mine and crept slowly behind her, as far back as I could.

Luckily Bree headed straight home. I knew the way well enough that I could hang back at a great distance, staying behind other cars. Once she had pulled into her driveway and parked, I pulled over myself at the very end of her block, behind a big maroon minivan, and shut off my engine.

Just as I was about to get out, though, Raven pulled up in her battered black Peugeot. Bree ran back out of her house.

I waited. The two girls talked for a while on the sidewalk, then headed to Raven's car and got in. Raven roared off, leaving a trail of foul exhaust behind her.

I was nonplussed. This hadn't been in my plan. Right now I was supposed to be talking to Bree, possibly arguing with her. Raven hadn't figured into it. Where were they going?

A sudden fierce curiosity took hold of me, and I started my car again. After four blocks I caught sight of them once more.

They headed north, out of town on Westwood. I followed, already suspecting where they were headed.

When they reached the cornfields at the north of town, where our coven had had its first meeting, Raven pulled off onto the road's shoulder and parked.

Slowing, I waited until they had disappeared into the recently stripped cornfield, then drove to the other side and hid Das Boot under the huge willow oak. Though the branches were almost bare, its trunk was thick and the ground dipped slightly so that no one casually glancing over would spot my car.

Then I hurried across the road and began to pick my way through the crumpled, messy remains of what had been a tall field of golden feed corn.

I couldn't see Raven and Bree ahead of me, but I knew where they were going: to the old Methodist cemetery where we had celebrated Samhain just ten days ago. Ten days ago, when Cal had kissed me in front of the coven and Bree and I had become true enemies.

It felt like much longer ago than that.

I stepped across the trickling stream and headed uphill into a stand of old hardwood trees. I went more slowly, casting my senses, listening for their voices. I didn't really know what I was doing and felt kind of like a stalker. But I had been wondering about their new coven. I couldn't resist finding out what they were up to.

When I reached the edge of the graveyard, I saw them ahead, standing by the stone sarcophagus that had served as our altar on Samhain. The two of them stood there, not talking, and it came to me: They were waiting for someone.

I sank down on the damp, cold earth beside an ancient tombstone. My face ached a little, and the stitch in my lip was itching. I wished I had remembered to take more arnica or Tylenol before I left the house.

Bree rubbed her hands up and down her arms. Raven kept pushing back her dyed black hair. They both looked nervous and excited.

Then Bree turned and peered into the shadows. Raven grew very still, and my heart beat loudly in the silence.

The person meeting them was a woman, or rather a girl, maybe a couple of years older than Raven. Maybe just a year. The more I looked at her, the younger she became.

She was beautiful in an unusual, otherworldly kind of way. Fine blond hair shone starkly against her black leather motorcycle jacket, and she had very short, almost white bangs. Her cheekbones were high and Nordic, her mouth full and too wide for her face. But it was her eyes that seemed so compelling, even from far away. They were large and deep set and so black that they looked like holes, drawing light in and not letting it out again.

She greeted Bree and Raven so quietly, I couldn't hear the murmur of her voice. She seemed to ask them a question, and her dark eyes darted here and there like negative spotlights raking the area.

"No, no one followed us," I heard Bree say.

"No way." Raven laughed. "No one comes out here."

Still the girl looked around, her eyes flicking again and again to the tombstone I hid behind. If she was a witch, she might pick up on my presence. Quickly I closed my eyes, trying to shut everything down, focusing on becoming invisible, on trying to wrinkle the fabric of reality as little as possible. I am not here, I sent out into the world. I am not here. There is nothing here. You see nothing, you hear nothing, you feel nothing. I repeated this smoothly again and again, and finally the three girls started talking again.

Moving a centimeter at a time, I turned and faced them again.

"Revenge?" the girl said, her voice rich and musical.

"Yes," said Raven. "You see, there's . . ."

A breeze rustled the trees just then, and her words were

lost. They were speaking so quietly that it was only by using my strongest concentration that I could hear them at all.

"Dark magic," Raven said, and Bree looked at her with troubled eyes.

". . . to wither love," were the next words to float to me on the breeze. That was from the girl. I looked at her aura. Next to Bree's and Raven's darkness, she was made of pure light, shining like a sword in the increasing shadows of the graveyard.

"Their circle . . . our new coven . . . a girl with power . . . Cal . . . Saturday nights, at different places . . ."

They talked on, and my frustration grew at not being able to hear more. The sun went down quickly, as if a lamp had been dimmed, and I started to feel seriously chilly.

I leaned against the tombstone. What did this mean? They had mentioned Cal's name. I figured the "girl with power" was me. What were they planning? I had to tell Cal.

But there was no way to leave without their seeing me, so I was stuck on that damp ground, feeling my butt and legs go to sleep while my bruised face ached more and more.

At last, after about forty endless minutes, the girl left silently the way she had come, with only her light hair visible when she stepped into the darkness beneath the trees. Bree and Raven walked back through the graveyard, passing within ten feet of me, and headed back out through the cornfield. A minute later I heard Raven's car belch and peel off, and two minutes after that its exhaust drifted to me on the evening breeze.

I got up and brushed myself off, anxious to get home to take a hot, hot shower. The cornfields were now totally dark, and I felt weirded out by the creepy scene I had just witnessed. At one point I was sure I felt someone's concentrated stare on the back of my head, but when I whirled, nothing was there. Running back to my car, I jumped in, slamming and locking my door after me.

My hands were so cold and stiff, it took me a second to get the key in the ignition, and then I popped on my headlights and did a fast U-turn on Westwood. I was scared and irritated, and my earlier thoughts of clearing things up with Bree now seemed naive, laughable.

What were they planning? Were they really so angry with Cal and me that they would turn to dark magick? They were putting themselves in danger, making choices that were stupid and shortsighted.

I swung into my own driveway, shaken and chilled to the bone. Inside, I hurried up the stairs and stripped off my wet clothes. As the hot water dissolved my chills I thought and thought.

After dinner I called Cal and asked him to meet me by the willow oak the next day after school.

# 18

# Desire

September 20, 1983

    Angus and I sat home glumly tonight, thinking about what we would be doing if we were at home and everything was as it had been. I can't believe no one here celebrates the harvest, the richness of the autumn. The closest thing they have is Thanksgiving in November, but that seems to be more about pilgrims and Indians and turkey.

    The summer was blessed: hot, quiet, full of long slow days and nights filled with the sound of frogs and crickets. My garden grew magnificently, and I was so proud. The sun and earth and rain worked their magick without my helping or asking.

    Bridget is fine and fat. She's a champion mouser and can even catch crickets.

    My job is dull but fine. Angus is learning some beautiful woodworking. We have little money, but we're safe here.

    —M. R.

"I guess you're wondering why I asked you to meet me," I said as Cal slid into the front seat of my car on Wednesday afternoon.

"Because you wanted my body?" he guessed, and then I was laughing and holding him tightly and he was trying to find a part of me to kiss that wouldn't hurt. I was ninety percent better, but my face was still sensitive.

"Try here," I said, tapping my lips gently.

Slowly, carefully, he lowered his mouth to mine and applied just the slightest pressure.

"Mmmm," I said. Cal pulled back and looked at me.

"Let's get in the backseat," he said.

This seemed like a fine idea. The backseat of the Valiant was huge and roomy, and we felt comfortable and private as the November wind blew against the windows and whistled beneath the car.

"How are you feeling?" he asked, once we were cozily settled. "Did that arnica help?"

I nodded. "I think it did. The bruises seem to have gone away really fast."

He smiled and gently touched my temple. "Almost."

I had planned to tell him about what I'd seen yesterday, but now that we were together, the words flew out of my head. Contentedly I lay against him, feeling his hands smooth my skin, and I didn't want to think about following Bree or spying on her.

"Does this feel good?" Cal asked, sounding sleepy as he stroked my back. His eyes were closed, his knees were bent, his feet propped on the side door handle.

"Uh-huh," I said. I let my hand roam up and down his firm

chest. After a second I undid the top of his shirt. I slid my hand inside.

"Ummm," Cal whispered, and he turned a little so that we were facing each other, chest to chest. He kissed me so gently and so softly that it didn't hurt a bit.

Then I felt the shocking, hot sensation of my skin against his and realized our shirts had somehow edged up so that our stomachs were touching. It felt amazing, and I wrapped my leg around his hips, feeling the tiny ribs of his brown corduroy jeans pressing against my thigh through my leggings.

As I pressed myself closer to him I kept thinking, He's the one, the one, the one. My only one. My *mùirn beatha dàn*. The one meant for me. This was all supposed to happen.

Cal pulled back a little bit, then spoke against my cheek. "Am I the first person you've been close to?"

"Yes," I whispered. I felt his lips smile against my skin, and he held me tighter.

"I'm not your first person." I stated the obvious.

"No," he said after a moment. "Does that bother you?"

"Did you sleep with Bree?" I blurted out, then winced, wanting to erase the words.

Cal looked surprised. "Bree? Why . . ." He shook his head. "Where did that come from?"

"She told me you did," I said, trying to prepare myself for the answer, to act like it didn't matter. Gazing at my fingers resting against his chest, I waited to see what he would say.

"Bree told you that she slept with me?" he asked.

I nodded.

"Did you believe her?"

I shrugged, trying to suppress the panicky feeling that was

building inside me. "I didn't know. Bree is gorgeous, and she usually gets what she wants. I guess it wouldn't surprise me."

"I don't kiss and tell," Cal said, considering his words. "I think that stuff should be private."

My heart threatened to explode.

"But I'll tell you this much because I don't want it between us. Yes, Bree made it clear she was into the idea. But I wasn't available at the time, so it didn't happen."

I frowned. "Why weren't you available?"

He laughed, brushing back my hair. "I had already seen you."

"And it was witch at first sight." The words just slipped out. I winced, wishing I could take them back.

Cal shook his head, bemused. "What do you mean?"

"Raven and Bree said . . . that you're only with me because I'm a witch, a strong witch."

"Is that what you believe?" Cal asked, his voice cooler.

"I don't know," I said, starting to feel awful. Why did I ever begin this conversation?

Cal was silent for a couple of minutes and very still. "I don't know what the right answer is. Sure, your powers as a witch are really exciting to me. The idea of us working together, of helping you learn what I know, is . . . tantalizing. And as for the rest, I just . . . think you're beautiful. You're pretty and sexy, and I'm drawn to you. I don't even understand why we're having this conversation, after I told you about the *mùirn beatha dàn*." He shook his head.

I was silent, feeling like I had dug myself into a hole.

"Could you do me a favor?" he asked.

"What?" I asked, afraid of what he was about to say.

"Could you ignore what other people say?"

"I'll try," I said quietly.

"Could you do me another favor?"

I looked at him.

"Could you kiss me again? Things were just starting to get interesting."

Laughing, wanting to cry, I leaned down and kissed him. He held me to him strongly, pressing me against his body from chest to knees. His hands swept over my back, my sides, and explored my skin underneath my shirt. I felt his fingers smooth over the small birthmark I have under my right arm, feeling its raised edges.

"I've always had that," I whispered. He hadn't seen it, but it was a rose pink mark about an inch and a half long. I had always thought it looked like a small dagger. It made me smile to think of it now: I could say it looked like an athame.

"I love it," Cal murmured, feeling it again. "It's part of you." Then he kissed me again, sweeping me away on a tide of emotion.

"Think about magick," Cal whispered, and my scattered thoughts couldn't comprehend his meaning. He continued touching me, and he said, "Magick is a strong feeling, and this is a strong feeling. Put them together."

If I had tried talking just then, it would have come out as gibberish. But inside my mind, his words strung together and made some sort of dim sense. I thought about how I felt when I made magick or gathered magick: that feeling of power, of completion, of being connected to things, being part of the world. With Cal's hands on me I felt a similar and yet very different sensation: it, too, was power and a kind of gathering, but it was also like a door leading somewhere else.

And then I got it. It all came together. Our mouths together, our breaths wreathing themselves together, our minds in tune with each other, my hands on his skin, his hands on mine, and it felt almost like we were in a circle, when the energy is all around, there for the taking.

There was energy surrounding us, wrapping us together, and my shirt was pushed up, my breasts against the warm skin of his chest, and we were holding each other tightly and kissing, and magick sparked. Any words I said then would be a spell. Any thought I had would be a magickal directive. Anything I called to me would come.

It went way beyond exhilarating.

When we stopped and I opened my eyes, it was dark outside. I had no idea of what time it was and glanced at my watch to see I was late for dinner.

Groaning, I pulled down my shirt.

"What time is it?" Cal murmured, his fingers already reaching for his buttons.

"Six-thirty," I said. "I have to go."

"Okay."

As I reached for the door, he pulled me back against him so I sat in his lap.

"That was incredible," he whispered, kissing my cheek. He gave me a big grin. "I mean, that was incredible!"

I laughed, still feeling powerful as he opened the car door. "I'll see you tomorrow," he said. "And I'll think about you tonight."

He headed back to his own car. As I climbed into the

front seat of Das Boot and started the engine, emotion almost overwhelmed me.

It was only late that night, when I was lying in bed, that I remembered that I'd never told him about the blond witch.

On Thursday morning the only parking spot was right behind Breezy, Bree's sleek BMW. I thought about how easy it would be for my car to crush hers, then I smiled wryly at having such a mean, unmagickal thought.

"You look different," Mary K. said as I carefully maneuvered my car into the spot. She peered into the passenger's-side makeup mirror and reapplied her lip gloss.

I glanced at her, startled. Had she seen me in the car with Cal yesterday? "What do you mean?"

"Your bruises are a lot better," said Mary K. She looked out her car window. "Oh God, there he is."

My eyes narrowed at the sight of Bakker Blackburn skulking around the life sciences building, obviously waiting for Mary K.

"Mary K., he tried to hurt you," I reminded her.

She bit her lip, looking at him. "He's so sorry," she muttered.

"You can't trust him." I gathered up my backpack, and we opened our doors.

"I know," my sister said, looking at him. "I know." She moved off to see some of her girlfriends, and I headed for the coven hangout.

"Morgan." Raven's voice reached me from a few feet away. I looked over to see her and Bree striding along beside me.

I didn't say anything.

"Your face is looking more normal," said Raven snidely. "Did you do a magick spell to fix it? Oh, wait, you're not supposed to, right?"

I just kept on walking. So did they. I realized Raven and Bree were going to follow me all the way to the east door.

Jenna and Matt saw us first. Then Cal met my eyes and gave me an intimate smile, which I returned. His gaze grew cold when he saw Bree and Raven behind me.

"Hi, guys," said Jenna, with her usual friendliness. "Bree, how's it going?"

"Peachy keen," Bree said sarcastically. "Everything's great. How about you?"

"Fine," said Jenna. "I haven't had an asthma attack all week." Her eyes flicked to me, and I looked down.

"Really?" said Raven.

"Hey, Bree," called Seth Moore. He loped up to us, his baggy pants long around his ankles.

"Hi," said Bree, making that one word sound like a promise. "Why didn't you call me last night?"

"Didn't know I was supposed to," he said. "Tell you what—I'll call you twice tonight." He looked jubilant at this clear sign of approval and shifted his feet, looking at Bree.

"It's a date," she said in a smarmy, come-hither voice that anyone with two brain cells to rub together would see right through.

"Knock it off, Bree," Robbie said suddenly. Everyone else seemed surprised, but I remembered the look I'd seen on his face that day in the gym.

"Whaaat?" Bree looked at him with wide eyes.

"Knock it off," he said, sounding bored and angry. "It's not a date. Seth, take a hike. You won't be calling her."

We were all staring at Robbie, whose face was set and stiff with dislike.

Seth met his stare. "Who the hell are you?" he asked belligerently. "Her dad?"

Robbie shrugged, and I realized how tall he was, how heavy. He looked pretty formidable and made Seth seem slim and young. "Whatever," he said. "Forget about her."

"Robbie!" Bree snapped, her hands on her hips. "Who do you think you are? I can go out with anyone I want! God, you're worse than Chris!"

Robbie looked down at her. "Stop it, Bree," he said more quietly. "You don't want him." He held her gaze for a long time. I glanced at Jenna, and she raised an eyebrow.

Bree opened her mouth as if to speak, but no words came out. She seemed almost mesmerized.

"Hey!" said Seth. "You don't own her! You can't tell her who she wants!"

Slowly Robbie raised his eyes and looked at Seth like he was an insect. "Whatever," he said again, then he turned and walked into the school building as the bell rang.

For one startled moment Bree watched him leave, then she quickly looked at me, and it was like old times when we could pass a wealth of information in one second. Then she turned, and Raven snickered, and the two of them walked away. Seth stood there, looking dumb, and finally turned and headed off, muttering under his breath.

"She sure can pick 'em," Sharon said brightly.

Cal took my hand.

"Yeah," I said, wondering exactly what we had just witnessed. "And they can pick her, too."

# 19
# Sky and Hunter

*March 11, 1984*

*We have conceived a child. We were not trying to, but it happened, anyway. For the last two weeks I have been trying to find the strength to have an abortion so this child will never know the pain that we have seen in this life. But I cannot. I am not strong enough. So the child rests in my womb, and I will give birth sometime in November.*

*It will be a girl, and she will be a witch, but I will not teach her the craft. It is no longer a part of my life, nor will it be a part of my child's. We will name her Morgan, for Angus's mother. It is a strong name.*

*—M. R.*

On Friday night Cal and I had a date. We were going to a movie with Jenna, Matt, Sharon, and Ethan.

Sharon picked me up—we were meeting Cal at his

house. At seven o'clock she pulled her Mercedes into my driveway and honked the horn.

" 'Bye!" I yelled, slamming the door behind me.

When I got to the car, I saw that Ethan was in the front seat, so I climbed into the back. Sharon roared out of my driveway and hung a fast left onto Riverdale.

"Do you have to drive like a crazy person?" Ethan said, lighting a cigarette.

"Don't you dare make my car smell like an ashtray!" Sharon said, spinning the wheel and stepping on the gas.

Ethan cracked the window and expertly blew out smoke.

"Um, Ethan?" I said. "It's freezing back here."

Ethan sighed and tossed his cigarette out the window, where it hit the street with a thousand tiny orange sparks.

"Now you litter," Sharon said. "Very nice."

"Morgan's cold," Ethan said, rolling up his window. "Turn on her automatic butt warmer back there."

"Morgan?" Sharon asked, looking in the rearview mirror. "Do you want the seat warmer?"

"No, thanks," I said, trying not to laugh.

"How about the vibrator?" Ethan asked. "Hey, watch it! You were two inches away from that truck!"

"I was fine," Sharon said, rolling her eyes. "And there's no vibrator in this car."

"You left it at home?" Ethan asked innocently, and I cracked up while Sharon tried to punch Ethan as hard as she could without having an accident. I wished they would just start going out, but I wasn't sure Sharon had even realized how much she liked Ethan yet.

Amazingly, we made it to Cal's in one piece and saw

Matt's Jeep already parked in the driveway, along with at least twelve other cars.

"Cal's mom must be having a circle," Sharon said.

I hadn't seen Selene Belltower since the night she had helped calm my fears, and I wanted to thank her again. Cal let us in, kissing me hello, and took us back to the kitchen, where Matt was drinking a seltzer and Jenna was on the phone to the theater.

"What time?" she asked, making notes.

Cal leaned against the counter, pulling me against him.

Jenna hung up the phone. "Okay. It starts at eight-fifteen, so we should leave here around seven forty-five."

"Cool," said Matt.

"So we've got some time. You guys want something to drink?" asked Cal. He looked apologetic. "We have to keep the noise down because my mom's having a circle in a while."

"What time do they usually start?" I asked.

"Not till ten or so," he answered. "But people come early, hang out and talk, get caught up on their weeks."

"I wanted to tell your mom thanks again," I said.

"Oh, well, come on, then," he said, taking my hand. "You can see her. We'll be right back," he told the others.

"Did you take the last Coke?" Sharon accused Ethan as we left the kitchen.

"I'll split it with you," was his muffled reply.

Cal and I shared a grin as we walked through the foyer and then through the formal living room and the more casual great room. "There is definitely something happening there," he said, and I nodded.

"It'll be fun when they get together. Sparks will fly."

Cal gave two quick taps on the tall wooden door that led to the huge room Selene used for her circles. Then he opened it, and we walked in. It was quite different tonight than it had been the night I'd arrived here alone, shaken and upset. Now it was aglow with the light of at least a hundred candles. The air was scented with incense, and there were people, both men and women, standing around chatting.

"Morgan, dear, how nice to see you." Turning, I saw Alyce, from Practical Magick. She was wearing a long, purple, batik robe, and her silver hair was loose and hanging around her shoulders.

"Hi," I said. I'd forgotten she belonged to Starlocket. Quickly I searched for David, the clerk who made me nervous. He saw me and smiled, and I gave a tentative smile back.

"How are you?" Alyce asked, seeming to mean it as more than just a polite question.

I thought. "Up and down," I said honestly.

She nodded as if she understood.

Cal had left my side for a moment, and now he returned with his mother. She was also wearing a long, loose robe, but hers was a brilliant red and painted with gold moons and stars and suns. It was stunning.

"Hello, Morgan," she said in her rich, beautiful voice. She took both my hands in hers and kissed both of my cheeks, European style. I felt like royalty. She looked into my eyes and then placed a hand on my cheek. After a few moments she nodded. "It's been difficult," she murmured. "I'm afraid it will be more difficult still. But you're very strong...."

"Yes," I surprised myself by saying clearly. "I *am* very strong."

Selene Belltower gave me an assessing glance, then smiled at me and at Cal as if in approval. He grinned back at his mother and took my hand.

Her eyes swept the room then, and she focused on someone.

"Cal, I want you to meet someone," she said, and there was an undercurrent of something I didn't understand in her voice.

I followed her gaze and almost jumped a foot in the air when I saw the same pale-haired girl that Bree and Raven had met with in the cemetery. My mouth opened to say something, but a tension in Cal's hand made me look up at him.

He had the most extraordinary look on his face. As best as I can describe it, it was . . . predatory. I barely controlled a shiver. Suddenly I felt like I didn't know him at all.

I found myself following him as he crossed the room.

"Sky, this is my son, Cal Blaire," said Selene, introducing them. "Cal, this is Sky Eventide."

Wordlessly Cal pulled his hand free from mine and held it out to her. Sky shook it, her night dark eyes never leaving his face. I hated her. My stomach clenched as I saw the appraising way they looked at each other. I wanted to scratch her, tear at her, and I drew in a shuddering breath.

Then Cal looked at me. "This is my girlfriend, Morgan Rowlands," he said. He called me his girlfriend, which was mildly reassuring. Then her dark eyes were on me, like two pieces of coal, and I shook her hand, feeling its strength.

"Morgan," said Sky. She was English, and she had an incredibly musical, lilting voice, a voice that made me instantly want to hear her chanting, spelling, singing rituals. Which made me hate her more.

"Selene has mentioned you to me," said Sky. "I'm looking forward to getting to know you."

Over my dead body, I thought, but forced my mouth to stretch into something resembling a smile. I could feel Cal's tension, feel his body next to mine as he looked at her and practically drank her in with his eyes. Sky Eventide regarded Cal calmly, as if she saw his challenge and would meet it.

"I believe you know Hunter," she said, gesturing to someone behind her, who had his back to us.

The person behind Sky turned, and I almost gasped. If Sky was daytime, Hunter was sunlight. His hair was a pale gold, and he had fine, pale skin, with some freckles on his cheeks and nose. His eyes were a wide, clear green, with no traces of blue or brown or gray in them. He was stunningly good-looking, and he made my stomach turn. Like Sky, I hated him on sight, in a primitive, inexplicable way.

"Yes. I know Hunter," Cal said flatly, not extending his hand.

"Cal," said Hunter. He met Cal's gaze, then turned to me. I didn't smile. "And you are?"

I said nothing.

"Morgan Rowlands," Sky supplied. "Cal's girlfriend. Morgan, this is Hunter Niall."

Still I said nothing, and Hunter looked at me hard, as if trying to see through to my skeleton. It reminded me of the way Selene Belltower had first looked at me, but it caused no pain. Only a strong urge to be away from these people. My insides felt hollow and shaky, and I suddenly wanted desperately to go back to the kitchen, to be just a girl waiting to go to the movies with my friends.

"Hello, Morgan," Hunter said finally. I noticed that he was English, too.

"Cal," I said, trying not to choke, "we have to go. The movie." It wasn't true—we had nearly half an hour before we had to go—but I couldn't stand another minute of this.

"Yes," he said, looking down at me. "Yes." He looked at Sky again. "Have a good circle."

"We will," she said.

I wanted to run out of there. In my mind I wildly pictured Sky and Cal kissing, twining together, wrestling on his bed. I hated the jealousy I felt about him: I knew all too well how destructive jealousy could be. But I couldn't help it.

"Cal?" asked Selene as we were almost at the door. "Do you have a minute?"

He nodded, then squeezed my hand. "I'll be back in a sec," he said, and walked over to his mom. I kept walking, out the door, through the great room, through the living room and into the foyer. Feeling hot and clammy, I couldn't face Jenna, Matt, Sharon, and Ethan just yet. There was a powder room down the hall from the foyer, and I locked myself in. Again and again I splashed cold water on my face and cupped my hands and drank some.

What was the matter with me? Slowly my breathing calmed, and my face, despite its lingering, faint bruises, looked pretty normal. In all of my life I had never had such a strong reaction to anyone. Ever since Cal had first come to

Widow's Vale, my life had changed with huge, sweeping movements.

Finally I felt capable of seeing the others. Opening the door, I headed down the hall to the kitchen.

But then my skin prickled. In another moment I heard voices in the hall, low, murmuring. They were unmistakable: Sky and Hunter. And they were coming toward me.

I shrank against the wall, trying to fade into the wood-work, and suddenly I heard a click and fell backward. Catching myself, I didn't fall, but gaped in surprise as I realized there was a door hidden in the hallway.

Without thinking, hearing the voices grow closer, I slipped farther into the room and closed the door with a tiny snick. I leaned against it, my heart hammering, and listened as the voices moved past, down the hall. I strained to concentrate but couldn't make out any words. Why were Sky and Hunter affecting me this way? Why did they fill me with dread?

Then they passed, their voices faded, and silence filled my ears.

I blinked and looked at my surroundings. Although I hadn't even noticed the door in the hallway, in here it was clearly outlined, and a small inset catch showed me I could get out again.

It was a study, Selene's study, I realized quickly. A large library table in front of a window was draped with a tapestry and held a display of various mortars, pestles, and pint-size cauldrons. There was a sturdy leather couch, an antique desk with a computer and printer, and tall, oak bookcases filled with thousands of volumes.

The desk lamp was on, providing an intimate light, and I found myself drifting toward the bookcases. For the moment I forgot that my friends were waiting for me, that Cal had probably returned, that we had to leave for the movie soon. It all went out of my head as I started reading titles.

# 20

# Knowledge

*September 9, 1984*

*The child moves inside me all the time now. It is the most magickal thing. I can feel her quicken and grow, and it is unlike any other feeling. I sense that her powers will be strong.*

*Angus is after me to get married so the child will bear his name, but something in me is reluctant. I love Angus, but I feel separate from him. The people here think we are married already, and that is fine with me.*

*—M. R.*

*Angus just came in. He found a sigil on the fence post by our driveway. Goddess, what evil has followed us here?*

Selene Belltower had the most amazing library, and I felt I would be content to be locked in it for the rest of my life, just reading, reading everything. The top shelves were so high that there were two small ladders on tracks, library ladders, that ran around the room on brass rungs.

In the dim light from the desk lamp I peered at the book spines. Some books had no titles at all, others were worn down, some were stamped in silver or gold, and some had titles that were simply written on the spine with a marker. Once or twice I saw a book whose title appeared only when I was very close: It glowed softly, like a hologram, and then disappeared when I looked again.

I knew I should go. This was obviously Selene's private place; I shouldn't be in here without her permission. But couldn't I just sneak a quick peek at a book or two first?

Did I even have time? I glanced at my watch, which read seven-twenty. We weren't leaving for the movies for almost a half hour. Surely no one would miss me in the next five minutes. I could always say I'd been in the bathroom. . . .

The room was heavy and full with magick. It was everywhere; I breathed it in as I inhaled, and it vibrated beneath my feet as I walked.

Shaking, I read book titles. One whole bookcase held what appeared to be recipe books: recipes for spells, for foods that enhance magick, for foods appropriate for various holidays. In the next case were books about spell making and rituals. Some of the books looked ancient, with thin, disintegrating covers that I was afraid to touch. Yet I longed to read their yellowed pages.

Looking around at the wealth of magick contained in the room, I thought of the Rowanwands, who were famous for hoarding their knowledge and their secrets. Could Selene Belltower be a Rowanwand? Cal had said he and his mother didn't know which clan they were from, but maybe this library was a clue. I wondered how I could get my hands on these books. Would Selene lend them to me? Could Cal borrow them?

The books in the next case were labeled *Black Arts, Uses of Black Magick, Dark Spells,* even one called *Summoning Spirits.* It seemed dangerous to even have such books in the house, and I wondered why Selene had them. I felt a chill, and suddenly I was even less sure that I should be in the study. I turned to leave, but then I saw a narrow display case, with glass shelves lit from below. Small marble cups held handfuls of crystals and rocks of all kinds and color. I saw bloodstone, tigereye, lapis lazuli, turquoise. There were gems also, polished and cut.

It was incredible to me to have such materials at one's disposal: The idea that Selene could walk into this room and have in front of her everything she would need for almost any kind of spell—it was just amazing.

This knowledge was what I hungered for, what I knew I had to work for. My parents' dreams of my future, my old, half-formed plans to become a scientist—those thoughts seemed like smoke screens that would only hamper me in my real work: becoming as powerful a witch as I could be.

I knew I had to leave, but I couldn't tear myself away. I'll stay just five more minutes, I told myself as I moved across the room to the other bank of bookcases. Oh, the covens were here, I saw. Shelf after shelf of Books of Shadows. I took one down and opened it, feeling like a lightning bolt might strike me down at any second.

The book was heavy. I put it on the edge of Selene's desk. Inside, the pages were yellowed and tattered, almost crumbling at my touch. It was an ancient book—one entry was dated 1502! But it was either in code or another language, and there was no way for me to decipher it. I put the book back.

I knew that I really had to get out of there and head back to the others. I started thinking of what excuse I would use for my disappearance. Would it be realistic if I said I got lost?

I moved sideways toward the door and bumped into a library ladder. Without knowing why, I climbed it. Up high, the scent of dust and old leather and decaying paper was stronger. Holding the ladder, I leaned close to the books, trying to read in the faint light. *Covens in Ancient Rome. Theories of Stonehenge. Rowanwand and Woodbane: From Prehistoric Times Till Now.*

I knew there wasn't enough time to read everything, to linger and savor and devour as I ached to. I felt tormented by the knowledge that these books were here and yet weren't mine. A raging hunger had awoken in me, a craving for information, for learning, for enlightenment.

My fingertips skimmed the book spines, lingering on ones that were harder to read. On one of the upper shelves I found a dark red unmarked book tucked between two taller, thicker books on early Scottish history. As I passed its spine my fingers tingled. I brushed them over it again, forward and back. Tingle. Grinning, I pulled it out. It was too dark to make out its title, so I climbed down the ladder and took the book closer to Selene's desk.

Under the desk lamp I carefully opened the book to its title page. *Belwicket* was written there in a beautiful, flowing script. I paused, the blood hammering in my ears. Belwicket. That was my birth mother's coven.

Turning the page, I saw on the overleaf an inscription:

*This book is given to my incandescent one, my fire fairy, Bradhadair, on her fourteenth birthday. Welcome to Belwicket. With love from Mathair.*

My heart stopped, and my breath turned to ice inside my lungs. Bradhadair. My mother's Wiccan name. Alyce had told me. This was her Book of Shadows. But how could it be? It had been lost after the fire, hadn't it? Could there be some other Bradhadair, some other Belwicket?

Hands shaking, I started skimming the entries. About twenty pages in, "The whole town of Ballynigel turned out for Beltane," I read silently. "I was too old to dance around the maypole, but the younger girls did it and looked lovely. I saw that Angus Bramson lurking by the bicycles, watching me like he does. I pretended not to see him. I'm only fourteen, and he's sixteen!

"Anyway, we had a lovely Beltane feast, and then Ma led us in a gorgeous circle, out by the stone cliffs. —Bradhadair."

I tried to swallow but felt I was choking. I flipped through more pages toward the end. Instead of being signed Bradhadair, these entries were signed M. R.

Those were my initials. They also stood for Maeve Riordan. My mother.

Stunned, feeling dizzy, I sank down into Selene's desk chair, which squeaked. I had tunnel vision, and my head felt too heavy for my neck. Remembering long-ago Girl Scout training, I scooted the desk chair back and put my head between my knees, trying to take deep, calming breaths.

While I hung upside down in this graceless position, trying not to faint, my mind whirled with thoughts that bombarded me so fast, I couldn't make sense of them. Maeve Riordan. This was Maeve Riordan's Book of Shadows. This book before me, the one that had spoken to me even before I touched it, had belonged to my birth mother. The birth mother who had been burned to death only sixteen years ago, in a town two hours from here.

Selene Belltower had her Book of Shadows. Why?

I straightened up. Rapidly I read passages here and there, reading the entries as my mother changed from being a girlish fourteen-year-old, newly initiated, to a teenager experiencing love, to a woman who'd lived through hell by the age of twenty-two, as she found herself pregnant with an unplanned child. Me.

My gaze blurred with hot tears, and I flipped back to the front of the book, where the entries were light, girlish, full of wonder and the joy of magick.

Of course this book was mine. Of course I would take it with me tonight. There was no doubt about that. But how had Selene Belltower come to have it in her library? And why, knowing what she knew about me, had she never mentioned it or offered it to me? Was it possible that she'd forgotten she had it?

I rubbed the tears out of my eyes and flipped through the pages, watching as my birth mother's spells became more ambitious and far-reaching, her love deeper and more compassionate.

This was my history, my background, my origin. It was all here in these handwritten pages. In this book I would discover everything there was to know about who I was and where I had come from.

I looked at my watch. It was seven forty-five. Oh my God. I'd been in here for more than twenty minutes already. And now it was time to go. The others were surely looking for me.

As hard as it was, I started to close the book. How was I going to get it out of the house?

Then the secret study door opened. A shaft of light from the hall dropped into the room, and I looked up to see Cal and Selene standing there, staring at me sitting at Selene's desk, an open book before me.

And I knew I had trespassed unforgivably.